BECOMING JEWISH

The Journey of a Lifetime

JULIAN WYATT

SWEETSPIRE LITERATURE
MANAGEMENT

(Baghdad, Iraq, Chanukah 2007)

Me and My Partner, Lisa, the love of my life (April 14, 2019)

Dedication

My Beautiful Partner, Lisa J.Stow-Wyatt
My Mom, Anne Kozdron, of Blessed Memory
My Jewish Mom and Dad, Lucy and Michael Sukman
My Siblings, Tanya, Jason, and Natasha
My children, Diana, Nicole, Daniel,
Gabrielle, Nathan, Alicia, Jackson and Cole
Jodie Lynn
Glen Bourque
Rick and family
My Grandchildren, Angel, Cameron, Sophia, Payton,
Addison, Natalie RosaLynn, Trey, Anniyah, and Jaden
All Servicemen and women, those considering
Becoming a Jew by Choice
and
All those that are struggling with Post Traumatic Stress

To B'nai Baghdad, in particular Maj. Stuart Adam Wolfer,
of Blessed Memory, his beautiful family and the living legacy
of the "The Major Stuart Adam Wolfer Foundation."

Thank you. Without your support and patience, I would
have never achieved my dream of becoming an Author.

"The wonderful thing about books is that they allow us to enter imaginatively into someone else's life. And when we do that, we learn to sympathize with other people," the gifted writer Katherine Paterson reminds us. "But the real surprise is that we also learn truths about ourselves, about our own lives, that somehow we hadn't been able to see before."

Or as the great Yankees Hall of Famer Yogi Berra so succinctly put it: "It's déjà vu all over again."

TABLE OF CONTENTS

ACKNOWLEDGEMENTS

I would like to thank all Rabbis that have mentored me throughout the course of my journey. *Rabbi Scott Gurdin*, thank you for making the impossible, possible. Thanks to your leadership and guidance over the years, I have developed a love of Judaism that has physically kept me alive. *Rabbi Andrew Shulman*, the memories of serving in Iraq and having you there to celebrate the holidays with B'nai Baghdad, was an experience I will never forget. It was you that helped me get my name on the list of Jewish service members serving overseas, that opened the doors to so many care packages filled with love, support and goodies. *Rabbi Nancy Myers*, thank you for the energy, passion and assistance with Anti-Semitic Harassment while residing in Huntington Beach. I adore your family! To *Rabbi Menachem Katz*, Aleph Institute, thank you for Lay Leader Support. You are making a difference in so many ways. To *Rabbi Dean Shaprio*, your friendship, guidance and love has been omnipresent. You have helped me in more ways than you can possibly know. Thank you to my baby sister, *Natasha*, Author and inspiration. Finally, to my wife, *Lisa*: you have shown me the meaning of Unconditional Love. I would not be here without you. I love you Mama.

Thank you to all friends, family, mentors, and shipmates for the support over the years.

FOREWORD

<u>We Remember Them; Yitzkor memorial prayer</u>

At the rising of the sun and at its going down,
We remember them.

At the blowing of the wind and in the chill of winter,
We remember them.

(Baghdad, Iraq, 2008, Remembering Major Stuart Adam Wolfer)

At the opening of the buds and in the rebirth of spring,
We remember them.

At the shining of the sun and in the warmth of summer,
We remember them.

At the rustling of the leaves and in the beauty of autumn,
We remember them.

At the beginning of the year and at its end,
We remember them.

As long as we live,
They too will live;
For they are part of us,
As we remember them.

When we are weary and in need of strength,
We remember them.

When we are lost and sick at heart,
We remember them.

When we have joy we crave to share,
We remember them.

When we have decisions that are too difficult to make,
We remember them.

When we have achievements that are based on theirs,
We remember them.

As long as we live, they too shall live; For they were a part of
us, As we remember them.

(Major Stuart Adam Wolfer of blessed memory)

My favorite book exploration invocation is:

"Divine Guidance is my only reality and Divine Guidance richly manifests for me in the perfect book at the perfect price. As I seek, I shall find, and I give thanks." I call this true self-help treatment "bibliotherapy," seeking Divine guidance through books, which is an ancient form of prayer.

Sarah Ban Breathnach, "Simple Abundance."

A writer is someone who completes the act of writing: a poem, play, short story, novella, novel, nonfiction narrative, biography, essay, script, feature article, a blog post. One really bad page. Or a terrible paragraph. Even a sentence. Heaven knows, I've spent entire days on one sentence: putting a comma in during the morning, then taking it out in the afternoon (Thank you, Oscar Wilde.).

Sarah Ban Breathnach, "Simple Abundance."

PREFACE

In no particular order, this book is my attempt to convey being a Jew-By-Choice (my learning experience), orders to Iraq as an Individual Augmentee, duties as a Jewish Lay Leader aboard Navy installations, combating hatred, my struggle with Post Traumatic Stress Disorder (PTSD), the loss of Major Stuart Adam Wolfer of Blessed Memory and my retirement from the United States Navy in 2010, completing 30 years of service. I hope you enjoy the book and that it gives you a glimpse of the life of a Jewish Sailor.

(Me and My Mom, Anne Kozdron, of blessed memory,
at Temple Sinai, Newport News, VA, 2008)

(Daily prayers)

A great Rabbi named Menachem Mendel Schneerson once said that "everyone should be involved in spreading knowledge. Even if all someone knows is one letter of the alphabet they should teach that letter to someone who doesn't know it. If they know more…well they should teach more! In that way we will ALL enrich the lives of others (Miiko Shaffier)."

INTRODUCTION

My story begins with being raised as an Episcopalian in Newark, New Jersey and fortunate enough to attend parochial grammar school and high school; Saint Charles and Essex Catholic High School. My parents both worked. My Mom, Anne, of blessed Memory, was in the Nursing Field and worked in Antique Stores. My Dad, Archie Wyatt, worked as a Medic in World War II and while growing up he worked at a major department store called Mangles in New York City during the day and in the evening he worked at the New York Times. He commuted from our home in Newark, leaving the house in the early morning hours and returning close to mid-night, 5 days a week. I suspect this is where I learned my work ethic and became so close to my Mom and oldest sister, Tanya. I am the second oldest of four siblings. I was born in 1960.

We attended church as a family sporadically, but in school, religious studies were part of the curriculum. I remember having a lot of questions about original sin, purpose of life, the New Testament and moral as well as ethical questions that seemed to always elude me. Hindsight being 20/20, I was merely following the faith on Sunday's and at school, but deep down, I was not connected, I didn't have the passion and I was not living and breathing Christianity. Oddly enough, from as long as I can recall, I've always wanted to be a Rabbi or Priest. For most of my formidable years, I was clearly a nomad. I spoke with my Mom about many different religions, and we explored them together through deep and enriching conversations.

The defining moment came for me when my father passed away suddenly and unexpected in his sleep at home in 1978, one year before my graduation from High School. My journey began with this event and continued until I became a Jew by Choice in 2007 and later, a Bar Mitzvah in 2009. After graduating from High School in 1979, I joined the ranks of the Merchant Mariners and caught a container ship bound for the Middle East for 42 days, the USCV Staghound. I had a "Z-Card" and I was employed as an Able Bodied Seaman, Steward's Department and an Oiler and Wiper. I earned my sea legs and this experience was the catalyst to later join the United States Navy. Our first port of entry was Haifa, Israel. I recall leaving the ship with a bunch of guys and as we walked through the streets, a big party was in progress, the doors flew open and I was literally pulled into what was a Bar Mitzvah for a young man that just turned 13. I danced and drank the night away with a group of people I had never met before and to this date, I have never felt more of a connection and sense of purpose. That feeling has only intensified over the years. Upon return to port, New York City, I went off to complete 1-Year of College at Worcester State in Massachusetts, where I was born. In 1980, I enlisted in the Navy with a yearning to return to sea, discover the world and hopefully return to Israel.

From 1980 to present, my quest to learn as much about Judaism is not complete. I am a Jew by Choice, I have had a Bar Mitzvah, I have served as a Jewish Lay Leader onboard many Navy and Multi-National Installations and I was on the Board of Directors at my Shul (Yiddish for Synagogue), at Temple Emanuel of Tempe, in Tempe, Arizona. Our Rabbi was Dean Shapiro. I am a Jew-By-Choice and I have finally traveled full circle in being identified as, being associated with and living each and every day as a proud Jewish Father, Jewish

Son and Jewish Husband. Above and Beyond anything else that I may represent, I am more Jewish than anything else.

I wish I could tell you that this book is all about happy times and self-discovery, unfortunately, it is not. My struggle with Post Traumatic Stress Disorder from serving overseas and losing a good friend, and in that loss, becoming an adopted son to his Mother and Father, Esther and Len Wolfer, a brother to his sister Beverly and Uncle to his bride, Lee Wolfer and beautiful children. The journey continues, the struggle is ongoing, each day is an opportunity to grow and learn more about my faith, blessings, and dialogue with my Rabbis.

I have had the pleasure of speaking with many Jews by Choice or those considering joining "The Tribe" and I have enjoyed it so much, that a biproduct of that engagement and conversations was another reason for this book.

The majority of bookstores that I have frequented contain a relatively small section about Jews-by-Choice and I've yet to find any that share experiences in the United States Military. It is my greatest wish that this book will add to the existing literature in this field. This is my story…

Hillel HaBavli Ben Michael (My Hebrew Name)

Robin and family

CHAPTER ONE

Letter to a future member of the Tribe

Monday Evening, May 16th, 2011
Huntington Beach, CA.

- 8:00 p.m.

Dearest Robin,

I hope and pray that this letter arrives to find you and your family in the absolute best of health and spirits. First and foremost, congratulations on your journey to become a Jew by Choice. I have always believed that if you feel that you are Jewish in your heart of hearts, then you are already a proud member of the tribe. The learning process and experience (conversion) simply makes it official. You will also be counted as part of a Minyan, which is a quorum of ten Jewish adults required for certain religious obligations and paves the way for your eventual Bar Mitzvah that I highly recommend. It was a life changing moment for me as well as my family.

This letter is in no particular order. The photo on page xv of this book was taken of me while in Iraq, performing my daily prayers in a war torn and cramped trailer. At the time, I was an active duty Naval Officer, Lieutenant Commander, serving in the International Zone in downtown Baghdad, Iraq, as an advisor to an Iraqi General and as one of the Jewish Lay Leaders for the prestigious B'nai Baghdad.

Without a doubt, my morning prayers have always allowed me to begin my day enriched with peace and it is my first encounter with holiness beyond opening my eyes and reciting the Modeh Ani (Jewish prayer upon wakening) while still lying in bed.

I could talk all day long about why I became a "Jew by Choice" but suffice it to say during my first trip to Israel in 1979, my life changed forever. In retrospect, growing up as a Roman Catholic after converting from being an Episcopalian, surviving parochial school (1st grade through 12th grade), I never felt "passionate" about my faith. I am a firm believer that in life, you have to be passionate about what you are doing, what you believe in and how you live your life. It literally consumes you, from the inside out, where it matters the most. Without passion, there is no zest for life; instead, you are just existing and going through the motions. That's how it was for me as a Catholic. Because of my religious denomination, I was part of that group, period. I'm not sure besides for going to Church on Sunday if I did anything else that identified me as being labeled as a Catholic. This was "my experience."

For as long as I can remember though, I had many questions about my faith and wrestled with several concepts that could not be answered to my satisfaction. A few examples included original sin, one person dying for the sins of another, the manner in which forgiveness of sins is conducted with a blood sacrifice, the idea that G-d (purposely hyphenated out of respect) could ever present himself in human form and then be killed, that the Messiah has already come, the holy trinity (more than one G-d), pagan worship and so much more. I suited up for battle and engaged everyone I met to explain those questions and others, but to no avail. It was not until I visited

Israel for the first time, started reading a few texts to include my very first book in the early 1980's by Lydia Kukoff, "Choosing Judaism" and then reading books on the Kabbalah (Jewish mysticism) where everything began to take shape and resonate deep within me. One could say that the faith found me and I did not find it.

An alignment with how I lived my life, what I believed about life's purpose, a feeling of knowing and belonging to a community, a Monchu or rather a family with a past, finally began to unfold. One of my first books on Kabbalah was "The Way" by Rav Berg. To date, it was and is still one of my favorites. It was during this time period that I also discovered Mussar and fell in love with its concepts of self-development and continuous process improvement. It is the best self-help book I have ever read, bar none.

When you become a Jew, you will be asked to choose your Hebrew name, but you will also automatically inherit the names of the father and mother of the entire Jewish people, Abraham and Sarah, neither of whom were born to Jewish parents.

I have never felt the slightest bit of awkwardness being a Jew-by-Choice amongst our people and this includes my Orthodox brothers and sisters. Actually, most of my colleagues are Orthodox and Conservative and I truly enjoy davening (to recite prayers) with them. I am accepted as if I was born Jewish, so you are in good stead my brother.

I enjoy so much about our way of life, our culture, our shared traditions, practices, belief, and commonality. The fact that our religion came second and that we were a community first and foremost is extremely important to me. We can have different beliefs even within our own community and still be Jewish. We are a community, a people first and foremost. Each and every day, we take ordinary events and transform them into extraordinary or holy events; by eating, reciting prayers, blessing our children, observing Shabbat, retelling our family album through major and minor holidays annually, washing your hands and even while using the restroom. Daily activities become an opportunity to be holy or divine. For the first time in my life, I identify with being a Jew. The way I lead my life, the way I eat, the way I pray, the manner in which I raise my children, my ethics, my moral compass, discipline, being a father, a son, and a husband.

Having multiple ethnicities: Native American (Nipmuck and Penobscot), Scottish, African American, Irish, etc., are distant second, to my identification and affiliation as being Jewish if that makes sense. *Ancestry DNA and 23 and me revealed I have Jewish lineage!*

Everything I do and accomplish in my life has something to do with my Jewish identity. I belong to that community in every regard. This is the essential ingredient that was missing in my life. I suppose this is tantamount to how a child feels that is adopted and finally finds his or her biological parents and discovers their siblings, relatives, and grandparents. Until that day happens, they don't quite feel whole, like they belong, but the second that they do, their life is changed forever.

I am reminded that every Jew and convert was present at Mount Sinai. Living and observing as we do, is our attempt to hold on to that feeling, of being in G-d's presence.

My Learning Experience

My learning experience entailed 10 components, yours may be similar, more or less: (1) Sitting down with a Rabbi to discuss reasons for wanting to become Jewish; (2) observing a full year of holidays and festivals; (3) attending Shul (Yiddish for synagogue) on a regular basis; (4) taking introductory Hebrew language and history classes;

(5) being able to read basic Hebrew from the Torah; (6) participating in local events, basically becoming embedded in the Jewish way of life; (7) going through the covenant of circumcision – also referred to as a brit milah (since I was already circumcised a drop of blood still had to be drawn and I almost fainted – I hate needles); (8) experiencing the mikvah (ritual bath) ; (9) having a Bet din (court or oral board) and of course, (10) being called to the Torah in a ceremony where you will receive your certificate and be forever known by your Hebrew name that the Rabbi and you will have already chosen.

My Hebrew name is "Hillel Ha Bavli ben Michael." The name was adopted from Hillel, the famous Jewish Leader who was born in Babylon, now Iraq, was a scholar and coined several phrases that epitomize our Jewish way of life: "If I am not for myself, who will be for me? And when I am for myself, what am I? And if not now, when?" "That which is hateful to you, do not do to your fellow. That is the whole Torah; the rest is the explanation; go and learn."

The Rabbi and I chose this name because of my love for learning, having several Masters' degrees and being a Doctoral Candidate at the time in addition to my journey to Iraq, the original Babylonia and birthplace of Abraham. The name Michael, comes from my adopted Jewish Dad, Michael Sukman. I asked him for his permission to adopt his first name as part of my Hebrew name. He was raised Orthodox. He and my Mom, Lucy Sukman, are true gifts from Hashem.

Michael and Lucy helped me with my Bar Mitzvah and whenever I need counsel, I turn to them. Mom Lucy would feed me peppermint patties as a treat, for pronouncing Hebrew correctly. Every Jew By Choice needs to have Jewish parents in my opinion. I love my Dad and Mom as if they were my biological parents. As I digress…The similarities in selecting my Hebrew name were chilling. Needless to say, my adult Bar Mitzvah was the highlight of my journey.

My favorite Web Sites:

Over the years I have amassed a huge library of textbooks and reference materials. I refer to them often for wisdom and guidance. A few of my favorites are:

http://www.chabad.org

http://www.aish.com

http://www.whatjewsbelieve.org

http://www.g-dcast.com (video display of each weeks Parsha –
an animated presentation)

http://www.becomingjewish.org/conversion.html (the 72
topics are awesome)

http://ccarnet.org/documentsandpositions/responsa/ For
Reform Judaism (Rabbinate)

http://www.jewfaq.org/index.htm

http://www.hebrew4christians.com/ (excellent for learning
Hebrew and reading Torah)

http://shamash.org/

http://www.uahc.org/

http://torahaura.com/

http://jewishlights.com/

http://www.mussarleadership.org/middot_table.html

http://www.msawi.org/About_MSAWI.html

https://www.mindfulnessfirst.org

My favorite 19 Books:

A few of my favorite books include:

— The Way, Using the wisdom of Kabbalah, by Rav Berg

— The Torah: A modern commentary by Plaut (I have a large one and small one)

— A handbook for people converting to Judaism and for their family and friends: Choosing a Jewish Life by Anita Diamant (this is awesome)

— What do Jews Believe by David Ariel

— The Modern Men's Torah Commentary by Rabbi Salkin

— Everyday Holiness by Alan Mornis (Mussar teachings)

— The Jewish Holidays by Michael Strassfeld

— The Jewish Book of Values by Rabbi Telushkin (day-by-day)

— A daily dose of Torah, the Kleinman Edition by ArtScroll series (there are 12 books with 4 weeks of Parsha contained in each one). Each volume contains a Torah thought for the day, the Mishnah for the day, Gems from the Gemara, A Mussar thought for the day, The Halachah of the Day, A closer look at the Siddur and lastly a Taste of Lomdus. Every day's reading for an entire week covers all 7 of those topics. The 12 volumes of the Daily dose of Torah presents a capsule study program for 28 days. It covers 52 weeks of the year and a 14th volume is devoted to Rosh Hashanah, Yom Kippur and the festivals. I love it!!!

— A time to every purpose by Jonathan D. Sarna (outstanding)

— Tanakh by JPS

— The Chumash by the Aleph Institute

— The Jewish Book of Why by Alfred Kolatch

— To pray as a Jew by Hayim Donin

— When bad things happen to good people by Harold Kushner

— The Jewish Way in Death and Mourning by Maurice Laam
— What Is A Jew by Morris Kertzer (core text)
— The Jewish Home by Daniel Syme (core text)
— To life by Harold Kushner (core text). Personal favorite.

Basic Judaism Texts: Recommended at my Shul:

(1)   Einstein, Stephen J. & Lydia Kikoff. <u>Every Person's Guide to Judaism.</u> New York: UAHC Press, 1989.

(2)   Klein, Isaac. <u>A Guide to Jewish Religious Practice.</u> New York: The Jewish Theological Seminary of America, 1979.

(3)   Knobel, Peter S.<u>Gates of the Seasons</u>. New York; CCAR, 1983.

(4)   Maslin, Simon J., ed.. <u>Gates of Mitzvah.</u> New York: CCAR, 1979.

(5)   Siegel, Richard, Strassfeld, Sharon & Strassfeld, Michaels, eds.. <u>The First Jewish Catalog.</u> Philadelphia: The Jewish Publication Society of American, 1973.

(6)   Strassfeld, Sharon & Strassfeld, Michael, eds.. <u>The Second Jewish Catalog.</u> Philadelphia: The Jewish Publication Society of American, 1976.

(7)   Strassfeld, Sharon & Strassfeld, Micahel, eds.. <u>The Third Jewish Catalog.</u> Philadelphia: The Jewish Publication Society of America, 1980.

(8)   Steinberg, Milton. <u>Basic Judaism.</u> San Diego: Harcourt Brace Jovanovich, Publishers, 1975 (N.B.: This classic was first published in 1947.)

(9)   Liturgy Committee of the CCAR. <u>Gates of Prayer.</u> New York: Central Conference of American Rabbis, 1975.

(10) Stern, Chaim, ed.. <u>On The Doorposts Of Your House.</u> New York: Central Conference of American Rabbis, 1994.

(11) Walter, Roy A. & Rosenman, Kenneth D.. <u>Gates of Prayer for Young People.</u> New York: Central Conference of American Rabbis, 1997.

Commentaries

(12) Fields, Harvey, ed.. <u>A Torah Commentary For Our Times,</u> Vols. I-III. New York: UAHC Press, 1990, 1991, 1993.

(13) Hertz, J.H., ed.. <u>Pentateuch & Haftorahs.</u> (Second Edition) Great Britain: Soncino Press, 1975. (N.B.: Any edition is excellent)

(14) Plaut, W. Gunther, ed.. <u>The Torah.</u> New York: Union of American Hebrew Congregations, 1981 (already mentioned above in my favorites).

Selected Books About The Hebrew Bible

(15) Ginzberg, Louis. <u>Legends of the Bible.</u> Philadelphia: The Jewish Publication Society of American, 1909, 1910, 1911, 1913, 1956.

(16) Heschel, Abraham, Joshua. <u>The Prophets.</u> Philadelphia: The Jewish Publication Society of American, 1962.

(17) Rosenberg, David, ed.. <u>Congregation.</u> USA: Harcourt Brace Jovanovich, Inc., 1987.

Additional Suggestions

(18) The Hebrew Scriptures by Samuel Sandmel (Oxford University Press, 1978)

(19) This Is The Torah by Alfred J. Koltach (Jonathan David, 1988)

Jewish Spirituality

*My favorite books dealing with Jewish Spirituality are written by Rabbi Lawrence Kushner of Sudbury Massachusetts. His books are distributed through **Jewish Lights** publishing in Woodstock, VT(802)457-4000). Titles include:*

The Book of Letters – A Mystical Hebrew Alphabet.

The Book of Words – Talking Spiritual Life, Living Spiritual Talk

Invisible Lines of Connection – Sacred Stories of the Ordinary

God Was in This Place & I Did Not Know – Finding Self, Spirituality & Ultimate Meaning

The River of Light – Spirituality, Judaism, Consciousness

Honey from the Rock – An Easy Introduction to Jewish Mysticism

Eyes Remade for Wonder – A Lawrence Kushner Reader

The Book of Miracles – A Young Person's Guide to Jewish Spiritual Awareness

A basic introduction to Judaism, mini course that I was exposed to encompassed bi-monthly meetings that covered the below format over a 6 -12 month period. This was in addition to Hebrew lessons where a teacher came in to teach an adult basic Hebrew class. Homework was required. Active participation was mandatory. Sit down sessions with Rabbi to discuss other items were required. This was a wonderful experience that only fueled the journey. The learning continues right up until today. I would hypothesize that every Rabbi has their own class curriculum, suffice it to say, having this format in advance can afford you an opportunity for self-study while you wait for that first meet and greet.

If you are considering becoming a Jew by Choice, I recommend finding a local Shul, attending a service, speaking with a Rabbi and jumping right in. Start with a Reform Synagogue and then venture out.

INTRODUCTION TO JUDAISM:
MINI – COURSE: PART I: JEWISH BASICS:

WHAT IS A JEW?

1. What is the Halachic (Jewish legal) definition of Jew?
2. Is there a common language that all Jews share?
3. Is there a common culture that all Jews share?
4. Are there physical traits that define Jews as a race?
5. Is there something biological about being a Jew?
6. Are all Israelis Jews? Are all Jews Israelis?
7. Can a person be Jewish and not belong to a synagogue or follow the rituals?
8. Are there conflicts with the definition of who is a Jew with the Orthodox; with Reform Judaism; with the State of Israel?
9. How might the word <u>unique</u> describe the Jewish people?
10. Are Jews and Judaism better than all other religions and people?

G-d

1. Is there a single, universally accepted Jewish statement about G-d?
2. Is there a creed or required belief in Judaism? (are there beliefs that are simply outside the scope of Judaism)?
3. Historically speaking has the Jewish perspective on G-d been static or evolutionary?

4. What role has Mitzvot (commandments, Jewish obligations) played in shaping the way Jews approach a relationship with G-d?

5. Is Judaism considered to be more "G-d centered" or more "people centered?"

Bible/Tanakh

1. Why don't Jews refer to the bible as the "old testament?"

2. What is the meaning of the word "Torah," in addition to "the five books of Moses?"

3. How is the Hebrew bible used in Jewish liturgy and study?

4. Is Judaism a biblically based religion? Is the bible the central focus of Jewish lore and practice?

5. What are the implications of the Torah being divinely given at Sinai? Does a Jew need to accept the bible literally?

6. Do Jews believe that the bible records accurate and true history?

7. What, if any, is the relationship between the Hebrew bible and the New Testament?

Covenant

1. What is a "covenant" (Brit) in Jewish tradition?

2. What does the term "chosen" mean in the context of the covenant?

3. What is the importance of this conventional relationship to Jews today?

4. How does a life which follows Mitzvot reflect the covenantal relationship?

Jewish texts

Talmud

1. What is the "oral law" and how is it different from the "written law"
2. The Talmud represents the rabbis' first formal effort to interpret Jewish scripture. What is the value and importance of such an effort?
3. What are the implications of the notion that the Mitzvot of the "oral law" are equal to those of the "written law?"
4. What role does the Talmud have in the life of a non-orthodox Jew?
5. Why is it important that disagreements and opinions are carefully recorded in the Talmud?
6. How has Midrash enhanced the texture and meaning of scripture in Jewish tradition?

Additional Jewish Texts: Commentary, Codes & Responsa

1. What was the impact of Rabbi Shelomo Ben Isaac (Rashir) in the area of Jewish idea thought, practice and theology?
2. How did the Rabbinic rules for scriptural interpretation affect and reflect the rabbis' understanding of Judaism? How did these rules manifest themselves in the various rabbinic commentaries of scripture?
3. How are the **Mishnah Torah** & the **Schulchan Aruch** different from the **Talmud**?
4. What are the implications of an ongoing rabbinic influence in the Responsa literature?

<u>Basic Jewish Theology</u> (an early comparison with Christianity)

1. Judaism and Christianity are fundamentally different in their respective approaches to the nature of good and evil. We will talk a bit about these basic differences.
2. Judaism and Christianity are fundamentally different in their approach to repentance and forgiveness. How do these differences shape the way we look at the human experience?
3. Judaism and Christianity have some very divergent views when it comes to their theological goals. What are some of these differences?

Introduction to Judaism: Part II:
Living as a Jew: Home, Synagogue, Community

<u>Home</u>

1. What are some of the essentials that define a Jewish home?
2. In what ways is the **mezuzah** an ideal symbol vis a vis the Jewish home?
3. Why is the home observance essential for a healthy Jewish family (and by extension, a healthy Jewish community)?

<u>Synagogue</u>

1. What are the various functions of the synagogue?
2. How does the synagogue compare to the church as a facility and institution?
3. What are the ramifications of being affiliated or non-affiliated as a Jew?
4. Are there differences between a temple, synagogue and Shul?

Community

1. What is the role of the Jewish federation in the Jewish world?
2. What specific organizations and helping facilities is a part of the Jewish community?
3. What is the meaning of **K'lal Yisrael** and why is it an important idea?
4. What role does **tzedakah** have in the life of a Jew?

Introduction to Judaism: Part II:
Living as a Jew: Family & Life Cycle Mitzvot

Family

1. Is the Jewish family inherently different from other types of families?
2. How has the Jewish family changed since the American immigrant experience?
3. Do the stereotypes about Jewish mothers, fathers, and prince/princess children really exist?
4. What are some of the basic elements involved in being Jewish parents?
5. How has the increased percentage of mixed and inter-marriage families changed the Jewish <u>extended</u> family and what are the implications?

Life Cycle Mitzvot

1. Does Judaism have any sacrament?
2. Can any Jew perform or be involved in the Jewish rituals?

3. We will speak briefly about the following Jewish life cycle events and observances:
    - Brit Milah
    - Baby naming for a Jewish girl
    - Pidyon Ha-Ben
    - Consecration
    - Bar/Bat Mitzvah
    - Confirmation
    - Wedding
    - Divorce
    - Funerals & Mourning customs

Introduction to Judaism: Part II:
Living as a Jew: The Jewish calendar

Shabbat

1. Why is Shabbat considered the holiest day in the Jewish calendar?
2. What are the basic Shabbat observances in the home?
3. How are the three basic components of Shabbat: **Menucha** (rest), **Kedusha** (holiness) and **Oneg** concretely expressed through Shabbat observances?
4. What are the traditional prohibitions that deal with activity on **Shabbat** and what is the value of such observance?
5. How does one conclude **Shabbat** and what is the significance of this ceremony?

The Three Pilgrimage Festivals

1. Why are Pesach, Shavuot, and Sukkot referred to as the Shalosh Regalim – the three pilgrimage festivals?
2. What are the biblical/historical, agricultural and theological components associated with the festivals?
3. What are some of the significant practices traditionally followed which are unique to each festival in both home and synagogue?

The High Holy Days

1. We will identify the two high holy days and we will look briefly at how they fit into a Jewish theological framework.
2. We will describe, briefly the basic home and synagogue observances and symbols associated with **Rosh Hashanah** and **Yom Kippur**?
3. What are the ramifications of being a "two time a year" Jew?

Minor Festival & Fasts

We will talk briefly about the major themes and observances associated with the following minor festivals (and fasts):

- Hanukkah
- Purim
- Tu b'Shevat
- Tisha B'Av
- Yom Ha-Shoah
- Yom Ha-Atzmaut

Introduction to Judaism: Part III: Judaism & Christianity

1. Let's view Judaism & Christianity and different religions from the same family tree.

    a) What is the relationship between Judaism & Christianity? (Sibling, parent-child, etc.)
    b) What "family traits" do Judaism & Christianity share? How do those "traits" manifest themselves?

2. We will talk about the word "Messiah"

    a) Hebrew term:
    b) Greek term:

To what did the original Hebrew term refer?
How did the rabbis of the Talmud change this original understanding?
How has Christianity changed this original understanding?
How has liberal Judaism changed this original understanding?

1. Do Jews recognize Jesus of Nazareth as the Messiah? As a prophet? Historical figure?
2. Who is responsible for the death of Jesus and what is the ramification of a Christian charge of deicide?
3. What are the specific similarities and differences between Judaism and Christianity regarding:

    a) Afterlife
    b) Salvation
    c) Rabbi/Priest/Minister

4. We will talk about observance of Christian holidays for Jewish spouses in mixed-religious households. We will look at some of the reasons why many Jews are particularly sensitive about these issues. We will also address how our decisions might affect our children.

Basic difference between Judaism and Christianity

Topics:

1. Definition of the word messiah.
2. Good and evil in people. How we atone for our sins.
3. Our goal in this world. How we achieve our goals.
4. What happens to us after we die? How important is this to us during our life on earth?
5. What is the bible? What is its purpose?
6. "Being" vs. "Becoming:" Christians must become Christian – they must do something or something must be done to them. Jews are Jewish. Most Jews are born that way. Nothing is done to them to make them Jewish. Jews who chose to be Jewish are Jewish forever.
7. "Doing' vs. "Believing."
8. "What happens to people who don't believe as we believe?"

In summary,

There are a few things in my life that I am most proud of accomplishing or discovering. Being a proud father, devoted husband to my best friend, a loving son and a proud Grandpa (Saba in Hebrew) to my grandchildren, is and will always be number one.

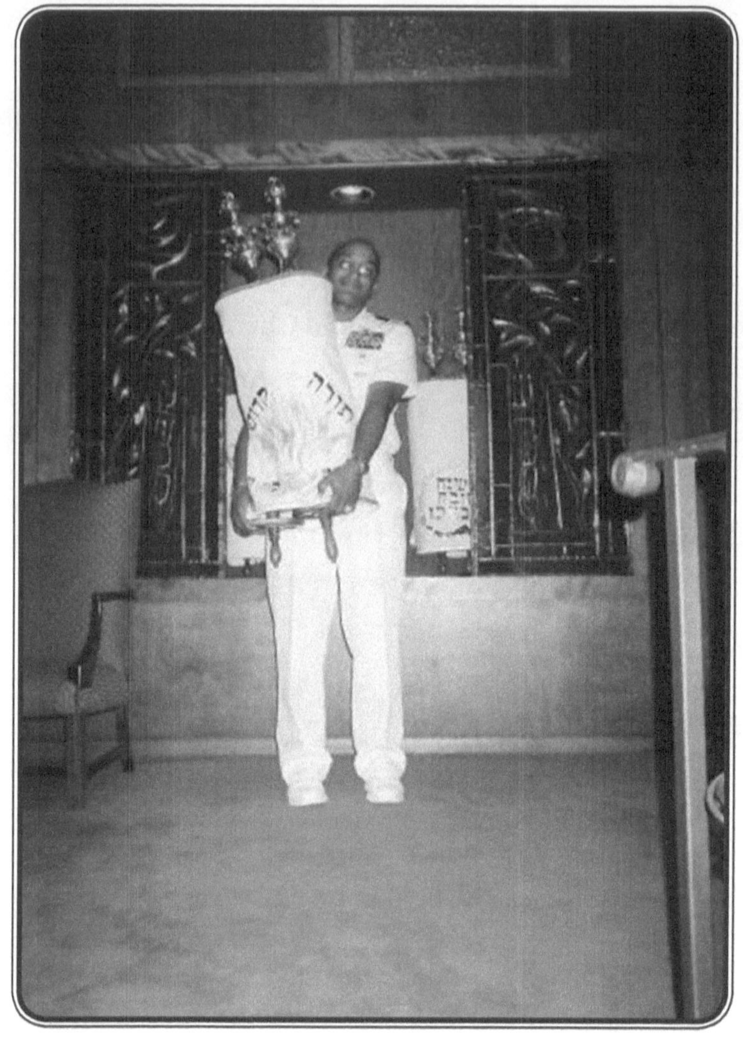

(2007, The ceremony, Virginia)

Becoming Jewish is number two. I'm inspired by your conviction, dedication and curiosity to become Jewish. If there is anything I can do to assist you in that endeavor, please do not hesitate to call upon me. Yours in shalom,

Your brother,
Jules

(July 8, 2010; Mom Lucy and Dad Michael Sukman)

(Me, with CDR Glen Bourque during my ceremony, 2007)

Me and Glen at my wedding; May 14th, 2019

Closing thoughts

I would not have changed anything in this process except perhaps having a Jew-by-Choice as a mentor or sponsor. I'm reminded in "The Second Jewish Book of Why" by Alfred J. Kolatch, "Judaism is not a race but a community bound together by religion, culture, language, and other interests. The bond that cements Jews is not blood, it is a subscription to a way of life that is far from monolithic. This is the reason converts are considered full Jews even though they came from non-Jewish blood. In Jewish law, anyone who adopts Judaism by choice is a full-fledged Jew (pg. 126)."

Master of the universe, I hereby forgive anyone who angered or antagonized me or who sinned against me—whether against my body, my property, my honor, or against anything of mine; whether he did so accidentally, willfully, carelessly, or purposely; whether through speech, deed, thought, or notion; whether in this transmigration or another transmigration....May no man be punished because of me. May it be Your will, my God and the God of my forefathers, that I may sin no more. Whatever sins I have done before You, may You blot out in your abundant mercies, but not through suffering or bad illnesses. May the expressions of my mouth and the thoughts of my heart find favor before You, my Rock and my Redeemer.*

"The nightly bedtime ritual of a Jew is supposed to include recitation of the Sh'ma, Judaism's credo statement. Prior to reciting it, one is supposed to read the above prayer. The prayer follows a commonsense formula of Jewish theology. First you forgive others for offenses they have committed against you; only then do you have the right to ask G-d to forgive you for offenses you have committed against him."

- Rabbi Joseph Telushkin, The book of Jewish Values

CHAPTER TWO

Orders to Baghdad, Iraq

The day when the Captain said: "Jules, the Primary failed the screening for Iraq as an Individual Augmentee (IA), you are the Alternate and you report to ECRC (Expeditionary Combat Readiness Center) next Monday."

It was a Friday, August 31st, 2007, when the Executive Officer and Commanding Officer pulled me aside and explained the orders and assignment. It was a hard pill to swallow but I knew quite a few people that left for an "IA." I replied to the Captain and Executive Officer that I would brief them next week on my turnover for duties as the 3M (Maintenance, Material and Management) Officer. I already knew who I would pick to relieve me, CW04 Danny Rogers. The only question was how to break it to my family.

I took a deep breath and called Lynn on the phone and asked how her day was going at work and what time she was going to be home. I needed to get a sense of how her day was evolving. We spoke for a few minutes and then I hung up. Later that evening, I told her I received orders to Iraq and that I was deploying in a week. You could cut the air with a knife. I had a lot to do in a short amount of time.

The ECRC checklist was extensive and included such things as Powers of Attorney, physicals, turn-over, packing, required courses and so much more. We did not go to Shul that evening. Instead, I called each one of my children, Mom and Siblings to break the news.

Later that evening, we were in the car running a few errands, and Lynn looked at me and said, "Do you have any regrets?" Is there any business that you are leaving unattended that you wish you had more time to complete? The reply took a few seconds and I said, "Yes, never having had the opportunity to become Jewish, especially after all the studying and observances over the past 20 plus years or so."

Well…that's all it took. Little did I know, she immediately got on the phone and called our Rabbi, she broke the news and said, "How can we make this happen in one week?" You have to know Lynn to fully appreciate her sense of resolve!

One thing led to another and on September 6th, 2007, my ceremony occurred. I remember everything as if it were yesterday. The Brit by the Mohel with Rabbi nearby in case I fainted.

Thank goodness I was already circumcised! The Mohel (the person that performs the actual circumcision) was phenomenal and quick. A drop of blood is still required as part of the covenant. The Bet Din (court) and the Mikvah (ritual bath), which was ice cold, was an experience like none other and the recitation of vows. I already knew the basic alphabet, all prayers and was observant. I also remember the long discussion with Rabbi about my Hebrew name, which was already mentioned in my letter to a future member of the tribe. A dream come true! The actual deployment was 436 days and was the highlight of my professional Navy Career.

(Fort Riley Kansas, 2007)

Two gifts were given to me at the time of my conversion: My Tallit (prayer shawl) on behalf of Lynn; and my Armed Forces Pocket Edition, Siddur (prayer book) for Jewish Armed Forces Personnel (my Dad, Michael Sukman). Not a day has gone by since, that I do not read from my Siddur and don my prayer shawl.

(Fort Riley Kansas, Prayer before Convoy Ops, 2007) (Training at Fort Riley, Kansas, 2007)

(Fort Riley Kansas, 2007, enroute to Baghdad, Iraq. From
Left to Right, LT Steve Wilkerson, CDR Charmaine Savage,
of Blessed Memory and LCDR Julian Wyatt - me)

Closing thoughts

For obvious reasons, there are many things I would have liked to have changed about receipt of orders to Iraq. A longer time to prepare for departure, and family services center counseling, especially for my children to help ease the fear and anxiety of their dad deploying to a war zone.

"Stories are like little time capsules. They carry pieces of truth and meaning over time. Whether it is a myth from 4,000 years ago or your own untold story from childhood, the meaning waits like a dry ration; only by the next telling does it enlarge and soften to become edible. It is the sweat and tears of the telling that bring the meaning out of its sleep as if no time has passed. It is the telling that heals."

Mark Nepo, The Book of Awakening

CHAPTER THREE

Jewish Lay Leader Duties

One of the first things I did was contact the Aleph Institute, under the expert tutelage of Rabbi Menachem Katz and I filled out a form that identified me as a Jewish Service Member serving in the Armed Forces. This did two things right away: My name became accessible to Shul's nationwide to send care packages and I received educational updates and information for free supplies for all holidays and as a Jewish Lay Leader (the person at the duty station that leads the services).

Albeit I can't speak for most in other services, but in the Navy, I never had a problem switching duty sections for the Sabbath, Friday evening at sunset to Saturday evening at Sunset. I did however stand a lot of duty on Sunday's! Likewise, being excused for minor and major holidays was afforded to me whenever possible.

When reporting to a duty station as a Jew, I recommend the following actions immediately, which includes overseas:

1. Find the Chaplain, explain that you are Jewish and ascertain if there are Shabbat services that you can attend.
2. If there are no services, guess what? You are it! Sit down with the Chaplain and order supplies which include Kosher wine, prayer books, supplies for upcoming holidays, candles, etc.

3. Order Kiddish cups, Challah, Matzo crackers, kippot, etc. The Aleph Institute is instrumental in this regard.

4. Find a location. You will probably share this space with other religious denominations.

5. Post flyers.

6. Ask the Chaplain if s/he can email individuals that have identified themselves as Jewish and put you in contact with them.

7. The Chaplain will list your name as a point of contact and can help with getting the word out.

8. If stationed aboard a Navy vessel, ask that the word be passed over the IMC (general announcing system), that Shabbat services are being held at the designated location.

9. Order various books as previously listed and a wide assortment of movies and games such as "Apples to Apples." Books on the various holidays are a must!

10. Work with the Chaplain on grief counseling and for Red Cross messages.

11. On the internet, I am a member of LinkedIn, a Professional Organization and I am a member of the Jewish Professionals group. I have queried many people, many of which are Rabbi's about everything from talking with military members about death and dying, to rituals and the like. A truly wonderful network.

12. My biggest challenge was maintaining Kashrut (kosher). I spoke with the people in the galley, in the Navy, Culinary Specialists, to see if they can always offer an alternative to pork and they accommodated to the best of their ability.

13. To those I was fortunate enough to lead in Shabbat services, I sent out a weekly Torah portion with commentary.

In regard to conducting service, it is best to lead a reform or conservative service. You must tailor the service to the median. A service that includes everyone. A typical service for me ran about 45 minutes and included response readings with all the basics touched upon; mandatory 6 psalms, songs and prayers. I was flexible and added others.

Many Jews that were not observant enjoyed the service and atmosphere. Our Oneg (meal after the service) to include aboard Navy ships, was enjoyed as a group with great discussions. Together, we shared interests, taught each other Hebrew, learned how to lay Tefillin (page xv) and so much more.

While on active duty, I wore my kippot, also known as a Yarmulke, every day with pride and so should you. The Department of Defense Directive 1300.17 regarding "Accommodation of Religious Practice within the Military Services" specifically addresses how a Kippah can be worn with a military uniform. I highly recommend becoming familiar with it and introduce the instruction to other Jewish Armed Forces Personnel.

(Various photos of Passover and regular services
onboard USS George H.W. Bush (CVN 77)

(Onboard USS George H.W. Bush, CVN 77)

I still recall the message on the Aleph Website to all Jews serving in the military and referred to it often: "Based upon a talk with Rabbi Joseph I. Schneersohn, the Previous Lubavitcher Rabbi of Saintly Memory, By the Grace of G-d, Elul 5704/1943."

Fellow Jews in the Armed Forces, in the camps, at the fronts, on land, sea and in the air! Listen to these words and reflect upon them, and you will, with G-d's help, gain courage and enhance the safety of your life and health.

Everything is in G-d's Hands!

You must know, dear brethren, that the life and health of every man is in G-d's hands. G-d guides the destinies of every man, and whatever happens to him, in all places and at all times, is predestined by G-d. If it is G-d's will that a person should live and be happy, that person will surely escape unscathed even under the most dangerous circumstances. Conversely, if it be Divinely destined that a person be harmed or die, that person cannot escape his fate even in the safest of places and under the best human care. This does not mean that one should be careless about one's safety. On the contrary. G-d has ordained that man should take care of himself, in the natural way, and, as our Torah tells us, no person should wantonly jeopardize his health or safety. For although G-d can save, in the most miraculous and supernatural way, any person He desires to save, very special merits are required for such Divine favor. Therefore, anyone placing oneself in danger for no good reason is foolhardy and deserving of the consequences, since in the first place, he can never know whether he merits such "special" Divine favor; and in the second place, by the sin of exposing himself to danger without justification, he minimizes his chance of a miraculous rescue. When, therefore, a person finds himself in danger, he should realize that it was Divinely destined so, and that whatever the danger, G-d can save him from it.

Moreover, precisely the dangers to which the soldier is often exposed give him an opportunity to see G-d's wonders at every step, and to become more firmly convinced how complete and absolute is the Divine guidance by which G-d takes care of each living being. Consequently, no man should lose heart under any circumstances. He should pray to G-d and trust Him to save his life and protect his health.

<u>All for You!</u>

You ought to derive much courage also from the knowledge that all your fellow Jews, men and women, young and old, all pray to G-d for your safety. Their prayers together with yours will surely be accepted.

Faith – the Basis of Confidence

The degree of hope and confidence possessed by a Jew depends upon the strength of his faith. The very faithful Jew is always full of hope, and consequently he is calm and courageous under the most trying circumstances. Faith is innately implanted in every Jew's heart.

Even the Jew who has strayed from the Jewish path by reason of a faulty Jewish education and upbringing, even he retains a spark of faith deep in his heart. This spark of faith may lie dormant for a long time until the occasion arises when it is suddenly kindled, and then it might well turn into a blazing flame of passionate Jewish faith. The occasion might be the revelation of some sacred truth of the Torah hitherto unknown to him, or finding himself in surroundings conducive to a mood of heartfelt prayer, or the performance of some mitzvah (precept), or any other occasion causing him to reflect upon his spiritual standard, and touching off that latent spark of faith in his heart. On such occasion he suddenly finds his intellect very clear and his heart overflowing with warmth, seeking expression in sincere prayer, earnest study of the Torah, careful observance of the Shabbos, selflessness and humility. These in turn strengthen his faith in G-d and in the Torah, and this faith breeds courage and confidence.

Jewish Soldiers!

Give your faith a chance to grow within you – and you will gain courage and happiness!

Some Spiritual Dangers

Let us now consider some of the spiritual dangers to which a Jewish soldier is frequently exposed, which we shall presently point out. However, like any other Jew who is given the choice of free will with regard to the observance of his religion, the soldier can and must likewise be the master of his will, and, with G-d's help, may overcome all spiritual trials confronting him in the course of his military service.

Of the spiritual dangers to which the Jewish soldier is particularly vulnerable, we shall mention but two general causes:

1. Being removed from his home atmosphere and finding himself in a new environment, often lacking adequate spiritual guidance, may have an undesirable effect upon the standard of his religious conduct.

2. Being obliged, in the course of his army duties, to disregard, on occasion, some Jewish law, the Jewish soldier might form the false impression that he is automatically absolved from the fulfillment of any Jewish laws, even when and where there is no military necessity to preclude him from their observance. Every Jewish soldier should bear in mind that a Jew must remain loyal to his faith under all circumstances and at all times, and that when he is sometimes obliged to transgress some Jewish law, he is not absolved from fulfilling it the next time.

You should remember, for instance, that you must not do any personal work on Shabbos, such as writing letters, sewing, etc.

<u>Your Opportunity!</u>

On the other hand, army life gives you an opportunity to fulfill some precepts of our Torah to a degree rarely afforded to a civilian. To wit, the precept of "thou shalt love thy neighbor like thyself," which, according to our great master and sage, Hillel HaZaken, is the very core of our Torah. In this point of love and comradeship which pervades our armed forces, forged as it is by sharing common experiences, common dangers, and by fighting for a common cause and ideals, you have a truly unique opportunity of helping your comrades-at-arms both materially and spiritually, and especially to strengthen the faith and religious observance of your fellow Jewish soldiers.

Dear Jewish Soldier, Marine & Flyer,

Take out [read] this message and reflect upon it, you will surely find the help of G-d, derive great moral strength from it and it will increase your faith and calm your heart. And if a feeling of apprehension or fear of the future sometimes creeps into your heart, G-d forbid, remember what we have just told you. Read this message over and over again, and let your religious conscience get the better of you.

It will be a source of renewed hope, renewed strength and fortitude for you. We wish you a safe and speedy return home, every one of you with a distinguished service record, both as a Jew and as an American. May we also merit the fulfillment of the prophetic vision of true peace and tranquility, when "nation shall not lift up sword against nation, nor shall they learn war anymore" (Isaiah 2:4), with the coming of the complete redemption through our righteous Messiah.

L'Alter L'Teshuvo, L'Alter L'Geulo!
Through immediate repentance to immediate redemption!
Originally published by Machne Israel
Second edition – Kislev 5727/1967

Website reference:
http://www.aleph-institute.org/message-to-jewish-military.html

Closing thoughts

The single most difficult challenge I faced was getting the word out and encouraging fellow military men and women to join in Shabbat services. The chaplains were great at providing my name to those personnel that self-identified as being Jewish.

Hindsight being 20/20, the one thing I would have advocated more strongly for, is interfaith services and being listed on the check-in and checkout sheet as the Jewish Layleader. Additionally, when we received American Red Cross notifications, I would have preferred to be notified of the death of a loved one that involved Jewish personnel, especially at sea! I would have been in a much better position to liaison with them directly and the family at a distance.

CHAPTER FOUR

B'nai Baghdad

I arrived in Iraq following 90 days of "Hooah Training" as an Individual Augmentee at Fort Riley in Kansas, December 10th, 2007, during Chanukah! The curriculum at Fort Riley was packaged in a "one size fits all" program and encompassed convoy operations, weapons firing and certification, language immersion, etc. My fondest memories were being embedded with multi services (Marines, Navy, Air Force and Army) and experiencing realistic simulations and scenarios that we would be exposed to once downrange.

My new uniform included desert camouflage, helmet, body armor (vest) with plates, boots, high tech sunglasses with gasket to block out the sandstorms, an M-4 rifle and M9 pistol with a combat load strapped to my vest. We lived 2 personnel to a trailer. My roommate was an Army Lieutenant Colonel, very cool. We were lucky in that our trailer had an adjoining shower utilized by occupants on the other side of us.

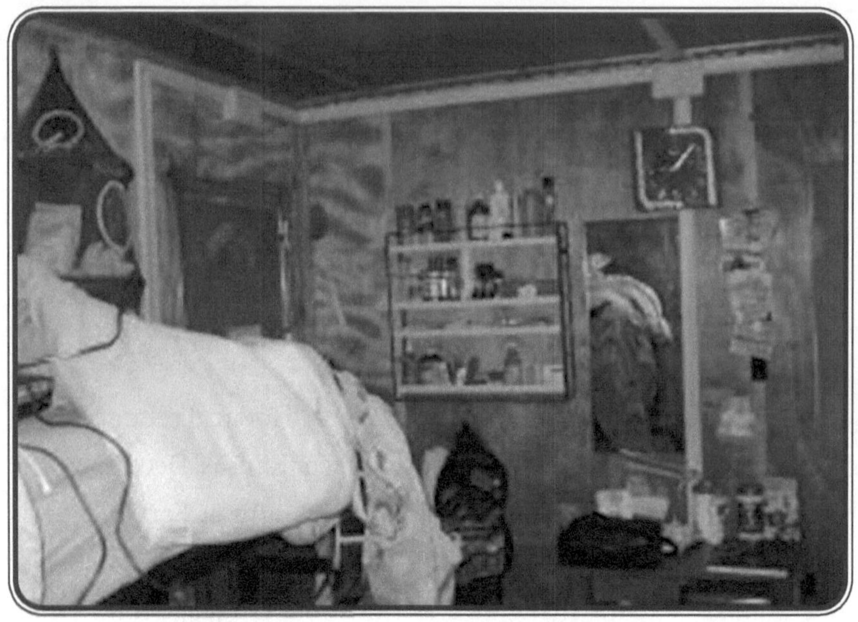

(Photos of my 2 man trailer in Iraq)

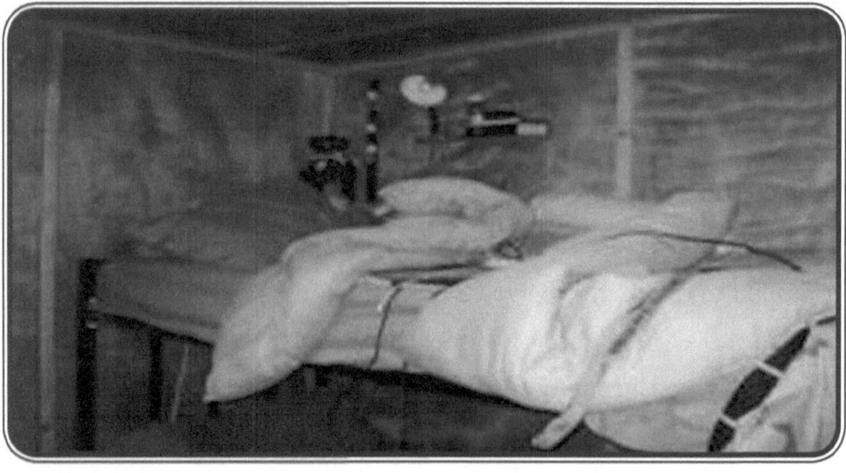

When I arrived in theatre, I contacted the Chaplain to ascertain if there were Jewish Services in the International Zone (IZ). He put me in contact with the Jewish Lay Leader, Major Elizabeth Robbins. I remember my first service as if it were yesterday! Our services were held in a trailer nestled in the compound of one of Salaam Hussein's palaces. The service always began with newcomers being welcomed and you told a little bit about yourself and family.

Our service lasted about 45 minutes and covered all the requirements of a conservative service. We utilized the Armed Services Siddur, the little black book. We took turns reading responsively. All chairs were arranged in a semi-circle with the Lay Leader on the end. The newest member read ***"the prayer for home,"*** which is one of my all-time favorite prayers:

"Far from home and those I love; I find my thoughts turning to them with affectionate longing. O God, You who are with my loved ones who are distant even as You are with me here, You hear their prayers even as You hear mine. Bless us and keep us united in spirit until we meet again. Let me so remember them that it will seem we are together and that I may be warmed by their love for me and my love for them. May my thoughts of those I love so move me that I will do them honor by my deeds even when I am far from them, even in strange and foreign settings. Dear God, keep me mindful of the blessing of their love, (my love for them and their love for me and Your love for us) that I may never yield to feelings of despondency, Help me to cheer my comrades who are also far from their families, their homes, and their loved ones. You, O God, are the Father of all, You are the source of all love. No one who puts his faith in You will ever feel forsaken. Amen."

The parsha (Torah portion for that week) was explained with questions posed to the group. Not everyone in attendance was Jewish! We ended the service with the Kiddish and Motzi and then proceeded to the Dining Facility (DFAC) for the Oneg and to play "apples to apples."

Unequivocally, I anxiously looked forward to Shabbat every week as a chance to break the chaos and constant shelling that surrounded us every day. The opportunity to pray with my fellow Jews, to laugh, cry and be a family was an emotional high point. During this timeframe I became acquainted with a local Iraqi Jewish woman named Khalida, that we would assist in securing safe passage to services.

We would take turns picking Khalida up each week under the 12th street Bridge under armed escort in an armored SUV and whisk her through the checkpoints and to service. To this day, I will never forget Khalida's courage and tenacity to go through Iraqi checkpoints and obvious harassment (her passport was stamped Jew), just to worship with us.

One of my colleagues that I would often walk home with after services was Major Stuart Adam Wolfer, of blessed memory. Stu told me that his wish was for Khalida to obtain a badge from the Embassy and eventually to leave the country. Stuart was not able to see his vision come to reality but it did happen, Khalida achieved a badge that allowed her safe passage to and from the International Zone.

I still remember the day that Stu joined B'nai Baghdad. He walked in, sat in the middle and was very outspoken. He introduced himself, spoke at length about his wife and girls at home, the farm and that he promised his Mom he would always wear his body armor and he did…even during our services where a majority of us removed our gear and kept it in close proximity. During the section in the service where we discussed the Parsha, Stu would often argue with the interpretation, not ours, but that of the actual scholars!

(Trailer where B'nai Baghdad held services – 2007 to 2008)

(Purim, 2008, Baghdad, Iraq)

I loved everything about being a member of B'nai Baghdad. Our close affiliation, shared values, beliefs and observances, kept me sane. I truly looked forward to a break in the hectic schedule called Shabbat, every Friday. But even more than that, just seeing one of our members on the base at the gym, on the bus, walking to and from facilities, allowed me to breathe just a little bit easier and keep hope alive. I can't compare this experience to anything else I have ever encountered, but I can say that I served in Iraq with my brothers and sisters and home didn't feel that far away...

(One of Sadaam Hussein's palaces where we had our Oneg, 2007-2008)

B'nai Baghdad (2007-2008)

Me and Khalida in Baghdad, Iraq at the Tigris river, 2007-2008

Closing thoughts

Nothing prepared me for my deployment to Iraq. The constant shelling and alarms which led to running into bunkers at a minutes notice, prevented restful sleep and forced you to contemplate death on a daily basis. I recall being in the Mental Health Field and facing death during my 12 hour shifts. We would accompany families into the morgue and prep the bodies by dimming the lights and just being there. Many nights when I came home, I would cry, hug my childrendearly and thank G-d everyone was safe. If we had monthly or quarterly round table discussions about how we felt, especially in regards to tragedy and death of children, would have allowed us time to heal this moral injury. That same format of discussions in a war zone, would have helped tremendously.

Window treatment at Blackhawk, the compound where I slept.

Easter Sunday, April 6, 2008, Baghdad, Iraq

(Attack on Phoenix Base, April 6, 2008; Photo taken by SGT 1st Class Jerry Saslav; edited by Jodie Lynn)

This is the email to Major Stuart Adam Wolfer's Family three days following the attack on the International Zone, Phoenix Base, Baghdad, Iraq, that took his life:

-----Original Message-----
From: Wyatt, Julian LCDR MNSTC-I DDA
Sent: Wednesday, April 09, 2008, 10:58 AM
To: Lee Wolfer and children
Cc: Mom Esther, Dad Len and Beverly, John and children
Subject: An honor and privilege to serve

The Year Two Thousand and Eight,
Wednesday Morning, April 9th
Downtown Baghdad, Iraq

- 9:30 a.m.
Dearest Lee, Lillian, Melissa, Isadora, Mr. & Mrs. Wolfer and Beverly,

My name is Hillel (Julian), I was stationed with your husband and best friend, father, son and brother. It was an honor and a privilege to serve with him. In the attached file, I am the only one with a dark suntan, kneeling in front (smile). Stu and I attended Shabbat, worked out in the gym together, spoke at length about marathons (I completed one back in 1999) and we were becoming very close.

On the day of the attack, I saw Stu at the gym; I was leaving as he was entering. My workout partner changed our start time, which ultimately saved my life. As I read Beverly's heartfelt letter, shared by Beth, I was moved to tears, yet once again. During Shabbat, we could always count on Stu to ask the "why" questions...he was full of energy, he embraced life with passion, zest and was always smiling.

I still recall the first day he attended Shabbat, everyone gives an introduction; and Stu spoke at length about his children, parents, his bride, sister, the farm and his career. I found myself leaning forward as he spoke, as if being drawn into an elaborate and beautiful painting.

What I would like you to know is that Stu was an amazing soldier, a compassionate friend and I consider him my brother. I am a better person after having known him and served with him. When we were alerted that Stu had passed away, 6 of us got together as quickly as possible, went straight to the hospital, were escorted in to be with him, and we prayed over him, reading psalms, standing beside him, all the way until such time as he was lifted into the heavens by the Angel flight helicopters. It was my distinct honor and privilege to be with him.

In our Navy tradition, when someone retires, we read something called "The watch." I have changed it, for a tribute in honor of Stu.
Yes, Family and Friends,
For many years, Stu has stood the watch.
While some of us lay about sleeping at night, Stu stood the watch.
While others of us were attending schools, Stu stood the watch.
And yes, even before many of us were born, Stu stood the watch.

For many years Stu stood the watch,
So that his family and friends could sleep soundly, in safety, Shelter and protection, knowing that no matter what, He would continue to stand the watch.

From all of his acts of kindness,
Role modeling how a noble man conducts his life, We are comforted knowing that a red rose is his sacred heart, A white rose is his face,

And that his breath has turned this barren world to a rich and flowery place.

He is the rose of Lee, his gardeners are we, and together, We shall drink his fragrance in the hearth of our love and memory, Where he will never die.

To his bride, I know he whispers the following words in her ear:
Darling, do not stand at my grave and forever weep.
I am not there; I do not sleep.
I am a thousand winds that blow.
I am the diamond glints on snow.
I am the sunlight on ripened grain.
I am the gentle autumn's rain.
When you awaken in the morning's hush
I am the swift uplifting rush
Of quiet birds in circled flight.
I am the soft stars that shine at night
Do not stand at my grave and forever cry.
I am not there. I did not die.

Today, we are here to say "Stu: Husband, Dad, Son, Brother, Friend and fellow Soldier, the watch stands relieved. Relieved by those you have raised, given advice, mentored, sacrificed and loved the only way you know how - gently and compassionately. Maj. Stuart Adam Wolfer, you now stand relieved, We, your family, friends and Soldiers in many different uniforms, have and will carry on the watch." With the deepest condolences and sympathy,

Hillel

I remember the day as if it were yesterday. I woke up at 0500, Easter Sunday, April 6, 2008, in my trailer which was nestled in the Believers Palace. The time was typical because I needed about 40 minutes to perform my prayers and complete the essentials. When I exited the trailer with body armor, M-4 and M9, complete weapons load out, goggles, helmet and work out bag, there was a sandstorm. I recall thinking that it was going to be a bad day. Typically, whenever we had sandstorms, the base received an increase in Mortar attacks.

I recall a few raids that morning with the piercing warning siren alert: "Warning, Warning, Take Cover, Incoming rounds!" The sound was louder than any fire alarm I have ever heard and I was use to hearing it. We were trained to get out of our trailers, stay low and proceed to a bunker as quickly as possible. The bunkers were scattered throughout the International Zone, every 50 feet or so and were cement enclosures opened on both ends. E-mail alerts also appeared which gave us another layer of warning.

To: DL MNSTC-I All Hands; IZ BDOC
Subject: ALERT WARNING U3 || INDIRECT FIRE IVO PHOENIX BASE || ALERT
WARNING U3

//////////////////////// ALERT WARNING ////////////////////////

* ALERT WARNING.
* TAKE COVER, TAKE COVER, TAKE COVER.
* ALL HANDS GO TO U-3 UNIFORM POSTURE.
* INDIRECT FIRE IMPACTING IVO PHOENIX BASE.
* THOSE IN HARDENED BUILDINGS REMAIN INDOORS.
* THOSE NOT IN HARDENED BUILDINGS MOVE
TO ALLOCATED DUCK AND COVER
BUNKERS IMMEDIATELY.
* REMAIN UNDER COVER IN U-3 UNTIL TOLD OTHERWISE.

//////////////////////// ALERT WARNING ////////////////////////

My typical work out time was around 11:30 with LT Bobby Page and ended at 1330 (1:30pm) at the Phoenix Base Gym. Bobby sent me an e-mail that morning and said that he had to leave early to work out because he was extremely frustrated with his supervisor (long story about that guy). I agreed and we met at 11:00 a.m. Around 1305 we were walking through the gym to exit and I stopped to speak with Stu. We spoke briefly about his workout, the sandstorm and I commented about getting my workout in early for the first time ever due to toxic leadership! We did a high five and as I departed, Stu was lifting weights in the back corner. Approximately 12 minutes or so later, the gym was struck by a 107mm Mortar. Numerous injuries and two fatalities. Stuart was one of them!

The next thing I recall was getting a phone call from our Jewish Lay Leader, Maj. Beth Robbins. She said that Stuart was fatally wounded and try to round up as many people as possible and report outside the CASH (28th Combat Support Hospital). Beth was calm but spoke with immediacy. She said to ensure we bring our Siddur.

Approximately half a dozen of B'nai Baghdad arrived. We were escorted into the Morgue where the Chaplain ushered us in and positioned Stuart in front of us so that we could see his face and ensure his feet were facing the door. We stood in silence for what seemed to be forever. Then Beth led us in reading Psalms. Stuart looked as if he were sleeping, very much at peace.

As a group, we acted as a Shomrim (Hebrew for watchers or guards). In our faith, when a Jewish person dies, he or she is never left unattended. Family members surround the person and pray for them until such time as they reach their final resting place.

We remained with Stuart for 2-3 hours as I recall. We were alerted to the incoming Angel helicopters that were inbound to pick up all fatalities and we walked beside the golf cart that carried our brother to the awaiting helos. I recall the walk back from that site to the palace where we sat, talked as a community and grieved. That next service was difficult and no one really knew what to say. Beth was the rock!

She kept us focused and we outwardly shared what only our hearts felt.

It was not long after the incident that we were contacted by Mom Esther looking for answers about what happened to her son. Beth shared an e-mail that brought everyone to tears. I emailed the family directly, which was the precept to this chapter. My relationship with the family continued long after that day and I was honored to have Beverly, Stuarts sister, attend my wedding and later, for Beverly, the children and Mom Esther attend my retirement from the Navy on July 8, 2010.

Every year, on the anniversary of Stuarts death, B'nai Baghdad assembles via a voice and visual chat and "we remember" our brother. We catch up on our lives, family, work and so much more. We end the gathering with recital of the Mourners Kaddish. In Hebrew, this is referred to as the "Yahrzeit" the anniversary of death that is observed according to the Hebrew calendar.

As is the case in all Jewish holidays, yahrzeit observance begins at sunset. A 24-hour candle is illuminated and, as a few of my colleagues have shared with me over the years, it is believed that the spirit of the dead fills the room once again for the 24 hour period." When I attend Shul, I offer Stuarts name so that the entire congregation can join me in this beautiful prayer.

יִתְגַּדַּל וְיִתְקַדַּשׁ שְׁמֵהּ רַבָּא (אָמֵן)

Yit'gadal v'yit'kadash sh'mei raba (Cong: Amein).
May His great Name grow exalted and sanctified (`Cong: Amen.)

בְּעָלְמָא דִּי בְרָא כִרְעוּתֵהּ

b'al'ma di v'ra khir'utei
in the world that He created as He willed.

וְיַמְלִיךְ מַלְכוּתֵהּ בְּחַיֵּיכוֹן וּבְיוֹמֵיכוֹן

v'yam'likh mal'khutei b'chayeikhon uv'yomeikhon

May He give reign to His kingship in your lifetimes and in your days,

וּבְחַיֵּי דְכָל בֵּית יִשְׂרָאֵל

uv'chayei d'khol beit yis'ra'eil

and in the lifetimes of the entire Family of Israel,

בַּעֲגָלָא וּבִזְמַן קָרִיב וְאִמְרוּ

ba'agala uviz'man kariv v'im'ru:

swiftly and soon. Now say:

(Mourners and Congregation:)

אָמֵן. יְהֵא שְׁמֵהּ רַבָּא מְבָרַךְ לְעָלַם וּלְעָלְמֵי עָלְמַיָּא

Amein. Y'hei sh'mei raba m'varakh l'alam ul'al'mei al'maya

(Amen. May His great Name be blessed forever and ever.)

יִתְבָּרַךְ וְיִשְׁתַּבַּח וְיִתְפָּאַר וְיִתְרוֹמַם וְיִתְנַשֵּׂא

Yit'barakh v'yish'tabach v'yit'pa'ar v'yit'romam v'yit'nasei

Blessed, praised, glorified, exalted, extolled,

וְיִתְהַדָּר וְיִתְעַלֶּה וְיִתְהַלָּל שְׁמֵהּ דְּקֻדְשָׁא

v'yit'hadar v'yit'aleh v'yit'halal sh'mei d'kud'sha

mighty, upraised, and lauded be the Name of the Holy One

(Mourners and Congregation:)

בְּרִיךְ הוּא

B'rikh hu.

Blessed is He.

לְעֵלָּא מִן כָּל בִּרְכָתָא וְשִׁירָתָא

l'eila min kol bir'khata v'shirata

beyond any blessing and song,

תֻּשְׁבְּחָתָא וְנֶחֱמָתָא דַּאֲמִירָן בְּעָלְמָא וְאִמְרוּ

toosh'b'chatah v'nechematah, da'ameeran b'al'mah, v'eemru:

praise and consolation that are uttered in the world. Now say:

(Mourners and Congregation:)

אָמֵן

Amein

Amen

יְהֵא שְׁלָמָא רַבָּא מִן שְׁמַיָּא

Y'hei sh'lama raba min sh'maya

May there be abundant peace from Heaven

וְחַיִּים עָלֵינוּ וְעַל כָּל יִשְׂרָאֵל וְאִמְרוּ

v'chayim aleinu v'al kol yis'ra'eil v'im'ru

and life upon us and upon all Israel. Now say:

(Mourners and Congregation:)

אָמֵן

Amein

Amen

עֹשֶׂה שָׁלוֹם בִּמְרוֹמָיו הוּא יַעֲשֶׂה שָׁלוֹם

Oseh shalom bim'romav hu ya'aseh shalom

He Who makes peace in His heights, may He make peace,

עָלֵינוּ וְעַל כָּל יִשְׂרָאֵל וְאִמְרוּ

aleinu v'al kol Yis'ra'eil v'im'ru

upon us and upon all Israel. Now say:

(Mourners and Congregation:)

אָמֵן

Amein

Amen

Acts of kindness such as demonstrated here, is another reason why I fall in love with Judaism, over and over again.

(Me, Rabbi Andrew Shulman and Maj. Stuart Adam Wolfer)

(A tribute to Stuart at the Gym, where he succumbed to fatal injuries.
I read the poem on Flanders Fields for family back at home, 2008)

(Phoenix Base Gym, 2007-2008)

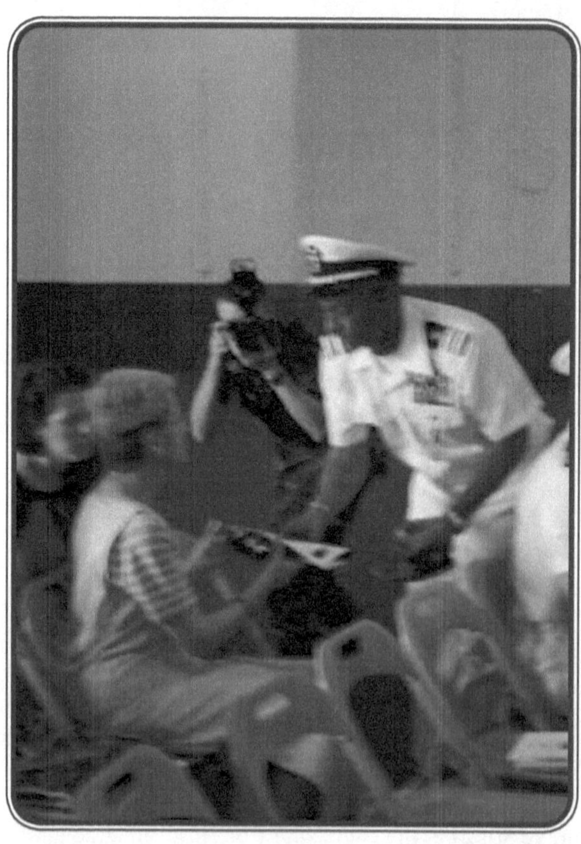

(Honoring Mom Esther with a flag at my retirement)

(Retirement Ceremony and Stuart's family, July 8, 2010,
Norfolk, Va. Me with Mom Esther)

In a way that honors, sustains and continues the work of Stuart, Mother and Father, Esther & Len Wolfer, and sister and brother-in-Law, Beverly & John Nerenburg, started a Foundation called the "Major Stuart Adam Wolfer Institute" and can be located at:

http://www.msawi.org/

On April 6, 2008, Major Stuart Adam Wolfer was killed in the Green Zone, Baghdad, Iraq. The Wolfer family will not allow Stuart's voice to be silenced. The Major Stuart Adam Wolfer Institute (MSAWI) was established so that his legacy of leadership, commitment to his country and community service will continue to live on and to inspire future generations of children, adults and leaders. The Institute is committed to supporting U.S. troops stationed overseas and domestically. The Institute seeks to directly involve the community in its mission so that those of us at home give of our most precious resource, our time.

The Institute seeks to increase awareness of the sacrifices our service people make on our behalf each and every day through educational programs at schools, communities and religious institutions. I emphatically endorse the Major Stuart Adam Wolfer Institute and recommend all Jewish Servicemen and Women that are deployed or about to deploy, to contact the institute to ensure your name is registered. You will receive supplies and care packages throughout your deployment.

Beverly, the children, Mom Esther and I, Navy Retirement,
July 8, 2010, USS George H.W. Bush, CVN 77

Closing thoughts

I'm not even sure where to begin beyond the information already provided. Prior to my departure, I communicated with my Rabbi and all members about the nature of my deployment. Lynn provided the mailing address for care packages on a monthly basis, she kept my organization at home up-to-date with photos and emails.

Linking up with B'nai Baghdad under the leadership of Maj. Elizabeth Robbins was a life saver and every Shabbat was so much more than just attending service. It was an opportunity to really freeze the moment, and to establish a community where we could sit, talk, yes pray and be as one. The ability to be amongst family in a war zone is priceless. A day of rest was an opportunity to reconnect and spend time with one another. B'nai Baghdad changed my view of what attending service should represent and what it truly means to welcome the stranger and establish a family.

CHAPTER SIX

Anti-Semitic Harassment, Huntington Beach, California and The Anti-Defamation League (ADL)

served 30 years in the United States Navy and 436 days in Combat. My safety and security is safeguarded by the sons and daughters of this great country that volunteer to wear the uniform. From July 2010 to August 2011, my family resided in Huntington Beach, California, where our safety and security were additionally safeguarded by the ADL. In our home the term ADL is synonymous with "Merchants of Hope." The mission of the ADL is clear:

> "The Anti-Defamation League was founded in 1913 "to stop the defamation of the Jewish people and to secure justice and fair treatment to all." Now the nation's premier civil rights/human relations agency, ADL fights anti-Semitism and all forms of bigotry, defends democratic ideals and protects civil rights for all."
>
> (http://www.adl.org/about-adl/)

We owe both the ADL and my comrades in Arms a debt of gratitude that can never be repaid. For those among you that have financially supported the ADL, I say thank you, because without that support, the level of assistance my family received could not have been accomplished. Specifically, the level of harassment required us to be relocated. It was the ADL through your support that paid for the U-Haul, the gas, the 2 months' rent and all packing supplies. The ADL was instrumental in getting the other family kicked out of the housing development and the boys removed from the school. The ADL was able to help us bring them to trial. The type of harassment included Lynn being verbally threatened at our home for alerting the school because the boys were in our son's class; Nathan was jumped and also verbally threatened at school by the Father and on April 27th, 2011, I was attacked with a hammer on a side street! Thank goodness I have three black belts. I held my own.

The harassment began with the boys in the neighborhood teasing Nathan about his "Star of David" necklace. They said he was a devil worshiper. At the time, my job in the Federal Government as a Program Manager involved me constantly traveling so a majority of the harassment was done without my physical presence. Lynn tried to resolve the issue with the children's mother, but it was futile. When I returned home I tried to speak with the father but the situation was explosive.

I was called racial names that began with the "N-word" and ended with the word "Jew" and a Baby Killer because of my affiliation with the Navy as a Veteran.

We filed police reports from our home when he came on our property to voice his contempt for Lynn bringing the school into the situation and when he threatened Nathan on school property, the school called the police. Please remember, Nathan was 11 years old and probably looked 8 and the individual in question, was 42. Attempts to obtain a restraining order was difficult because we could not obtain his home address. He was not residing permanently with his family in our complex.

I suspect the abuse was going on for 6-7 months when we finally mentioned it to our Rabbi. I'm not sure why we didn't say anything sooner. Rabbi told us to contact the ADL immediately and from that day forward, life became much easier. A personal advocate was assigned to our family. The Regional Director, Dr. Kevin O'Grady was phenomenal. Kevin met with us weekly, made phone calls and pressed people for copies of everything. Kevin and our personal advocate sat in court with us!

I remember going to LinkedIn where I have an account and posting a blog on the Jewish Professionals group detailing our experience. The outpouring of support, advice, counsel and personal contact information for Lawyers, etc., was above and beyond the call. Many of the people that I networked with are still friends to this day.

Interestingly, when I was active duty, when the ship arrived in a foreign port, we would receive a threat assessment that told us which places to stay clear of based on threats to servicemen and women. Shore patrol would frequent those establishments during liberty and if you were caught inside, you were brought back to the ship and held accountable. In the civilian world, that responsibility resides on the individual.

The decision to move to Huntington Beach was based on close proximity to good schools and my work at Seal Beach. I never thought for a minute to contact the ADL about Anti-Semitic Harassment. We did look at the crime rate in Huntington Beach and found it to be safe for our family. When the dust settled and we spoke with the detectives covering the case, the words echo in my ears "You could not have moved to a worse area."

I am a huge advocate and spokesperson for the ADL. If you have not taken the time to contact the local office to find out what's happening in your neighborhood or invited them to come and speak at your school, at your house of worship, an event or at your organization, I highly recommend it.

The ADL has a myriad of programs that may be of interest. One in particular is the designation "No Place For Hate." I was employed at a school that completed this program which provides a safer environment for our youth and it was free!

Ralph Waldo Emerson was spot on when he said: "To know that one person has breathed easier because you have lived, is to have achieved success." Mr. Bill Straus, Regional Director of the ADL in Phoenix, Arizona and Dr. Kevin O'Grady, Regional Director of Orange County have made a difference and enabled our family to breathe just a little bit easier. Thank you for all that you do and continue to do in repairing our world. Tikkun O'lam.

Closing thoughts

Of particular mention is Melissa Medvin, she was the program Coordinator for "No Place For Hate." Melissa was instrumental in providing one on one mentorship during the process which included all project planning, reports and final ceremony preparations. Anitbullying initiatives are desperately in need. The ADL can provide training, resources and materials to help you, the community and school to live a safer and hostile free environment.

CHAPTER SEVEN

Chanukah

Chanukah is one of our absolute favorite holiday seasons because of the history and message that it contains biblically and for us as a couple. The script that we follow is an old one and originated from the "United Jewish Community of the Virginia Peninsula" in Newport News, Virginia. I will share that process with you and perhaps you can utilize this program as you kindle the Chanukah lights. The text that accompanies the blessings is from "The Jewish Holiday's" by Michel Strassfeld. Before any holiday, I always read the appropriate section/chapter in that book and of course Jonathan D. Sarna "A time to every purpose."

1. Opening Prayer
2. Lighting the Shamash
3. Recitation of Chanukah blessings
4. Lighting of candles
5. Discuss meaning of "day," Exchange gifts, Songs, Psalms and Biblical passage
6. Closing prayer

Chanukah Blessings

(1) Baruch ata Adonai elohaynu melech ha-olam, asher kid'sha-nu b'mitz-vo-tav vitzi-vanu l'hadlik ner shel Chanukah. (Blessed are you, O Lord our G-d, Ruling Spirit of the Universe, who has sanctified us with His commandments, and has commanded us to kindle the Chanukah lights).

According to Strassfeld (1985, p. 167) after the lighting is completed, some people recite the *ha-neirot hallalu* paragraph: "We kindle these lights to commemorate the miracles, wonders, triumphs, and victories which You performed through Your holy priests for our ancestors in those days, in this season. These lights are sacred for all eight days of Chanukah. It is forbidden to make any use of them except to look at them in order to praise Your miracles, wonders and triumphs."

(2) Baruch ata Adonai elohaynu melech ha-olam, she'asa ni'sim lo'avotaynu ba'yamim ha'hem baz'man hazeh. (Blessed are you, O Lord our G-d, Ruling spirit of the Universe who has inspired the heroic deeds of our ancestors in times past at this season).

<u>First Night Only</u>

Baruch ata Adonai elohaynu melech ha-olam, she'he'che'ya'nu v'ki-y ma'nu v'hi'gi'anu laz man ha'zeh. (Blessed are You, O Lord our G-d, Ruling Spirit of the Universe, who has kept us alive, sustained us, and brought us to this season).

<u>FIRST NIGHT – FREEDOM</u>

<u>OPENING PRAYER</u>...We kindle these Chanukah lights in memory of the dedication and courage of the Maccabees. Believing that they should be free to worship G-d as their hearts and minds dictated, they willingly gave their lives for freedom. Now, kindling these candles, we rededicate ourselves to work for the equal rights of all people, and for the realization of a society of democracy and freedom.

LIGHT SHAMASH, RECITE BLESSINGS, LIGHT CANDLE

Baruch ata Adonai elohaynu melech ha-olam, asher kid'sha-nu b'mitz-vo-tav vitzi-vanu l'hadlik ner shel Chanukah. (Blessed are you, O Lord our G-d, Ruling Spirit of the Universe, who has sanctified us with His commandments, and has commanded us to kindle the Chanukah lights). "We kindle these lights to commemorate the miracles, wonders, triumphs, and victories which You performed through Your holy priests for our ancestors in those days, in this season. These lights are sacred for all eight days of Chanukah. It is forbidden to make any use of them except to look at them in order to praise Your miracles, wonders and triumphs."

Baruch ata Adonai elohaynu melech ha-olam, she'asa ni'sim lo'avotaynu ba'yamim ha'hem baz'man hazeh. (Blessed are you, O Lord our G-d, Ruling spirit of the Universe who has inspired the heroic deeds of our ancestors in times past at this season).

— Take turns around the table with each person talking about what freedom means to them. We make a special point of thanking the military for our freedom and we often set aside a plate at our table for all Jewish Servicemen and Women that are not at home with their families.
— Many people sing "Ma'oz tzur." (Recommend You-Tube and have this ready to play)

— Gifts are exchanged, Chanukah gelt is given and we play the game of the Dreidel.

— Psalms 30 and Psalm 44:2-9 is often recited

Psalm 30 (select a reader)

I will exalt you, Lord, for you lifted me out of the depths and did not let my enemies gloat over me. Lord my God, I called to you for help, and you healed me. You, Lord, brought me up from the realm of the dead; you spared me from going down to the pit. Sing the praises of the Lord, you his faithful people; praise his holy name. For his anger lasts only a moment, but his favor lasts a lifetime; weeping may stay for the night, but rejoicing comes in the morning. When I felt secure, I said, "I will never be shaken." Lord, when you favored me, you made my royal mountain[c] stand firm; but when you hid your face, I was dismayed. To you, Lord, I called; to the Lord I cried for mercy: "What is gained if I am silenced, if I go down to the pit? Will the dust praise you? Will it proclaim your faithfulness? Hear, Lord, and be merciful to me;

Lord, be my help." You turned my wailing into dancing; you removed my sackcloth and clothed me with joy, that my heart may sing your praises and not be silent. Lord my God, I will praise you forever.

Psalm 44: 2-9 (select a reader)

"With your hand you drove out the nations and planted our ancestors; you crushed the peoples and made our ancestors flourish. It was not by their sword that they won the land, nor did their arm bring them victory; it was your right hand, your arm, and the light of your face, for you loved them. You are my King and my God, who decrees victories for Jacob. Through you we push back our enemies; through your name we trample our foes. I put no trust in my bow, my sword does not bring me victory; but you give us victory over our enemies, you put our adversaries to shame. In God we make our boast all day long, and we will praise your name forever. But now you have rejected and humbled us; you no longer go out with our armies."

Biblical passage for FIRST NIGHT (select a reader)

The earth was unformed and void, with darkness over the surface of the deep…G-d said, "Let there be light,' and there was light. G-d saw that the light was good, and G-d separated the light from the darkness. G-d called the light Day, and the darkness He called Night…G-d said, "Let there be lights in the expanse of the sky to separate day from night; they shall serve as signs for the set times – the days and the years; and they shall serve as lights in the expanse of the sky to shine upon the earth." And it was so. G-d made the two great lights, the greater light to dominate the day and the lesser light to dominate the night, and the stars. And G-d set them in the expanse of the sky to shine upon the earth, to dominate the day and the night, and to separate light from darkness. And G-d saw that this was good (Gen. 1:2-5; 14-18).

<u>CLOSING PRAYER</u>…Our G-d and G-d of our ancestors, on this eve of Chanukah we rededicate ourselves to Thee. Let these lights shine forth brightly, reminding us that all people are created equal in thy sight. Inspire us anew, that we may serve the cause of freedom as valiantly as did our ancestors before us. Praised art Thou, O Lord who has implanted within us the love of freedom. AMEN.

<u>SECOND NIGHT – FAMILY</u>

<u>OPENING PRAYER</u>…Tonight as we celebrate Chanukah together, we are conscious of our precious gift of family. So often we take one another for granted, forgetting to express our love and devotion. Let us now, as we kindle these festive lights, rededicate ourselves to sharing our interests and time with one another. Like the Maccabees of old, let us always face the tribulations and the joys of life united by our family bonds. Kindling these lights, we pray that through kindness and thoughtfulness our love for each other will increase from strength to strength.

LIGHT SHAMASH, RECITE BLESSINGS, LIGHT CANDLE

Baruch ata Adonai elohaynu melech ha-olam, asher kid'sha-nu b'mitz-vo-tav vitzi-vanu l'hadlik ner shel Chanukah. (Blessed are you, O Lord our G-d, Ruling Spirit of the Universe, who has sanctified us with His commandments, and has commanded us to kindle the Chanukah lights). "We kindle these lights to commemorate the miracles, wonders, triumphs, and victories which You performed through Your holy priests for our ancestors in those days, in this season. These lights are sacred for all eight days of Chanukah. It is forbidden to make any use of them except to look at them in order to praise Your miracles, wonders and triumphs."

Baruch ata Adonai elohaynu melech ha-olam, she'asa ni'sim lo'avotaynu ba'yamim ha'hem baz'man hazeh. (Blessed are you, O Lord our G-d, Ruling spirit of the Universe who has inspired the heroic deeds of our ancestors in times past at this season).

— Take turns around the table with each person talking about what family means to them.

— Gifts are exchanged

Biblical passage for SECOND NIGHT (select a reader)

Woe to those who call evil good and good evil; who present darkness as light and light as darkness; who present bitter as sweet and sweet as bitter! Woe to those who are so wise – in their own opinion; So clever in their own judgment! Woe to those who are so heroic – as drinkers of wine, and so valiant – as mixers of drink! Who vindicate him who is in the wrong in return for a bride, and withhold vindication from him who is right. Assuredly, as straw is consumed by a tongue of fire and hay shrivels as it burns, their stock shall become like rot, and their buds shall blow away like dust. For they have rejected the instruction of the Lord of Hosts, spurned the word of the Holy One of Israel (Isa. 5:20-24).

<u>CLOSING PRAYER</u>…Eternal our G-d, we give thanks to you for preserving us in health and joy. We pray that all families everywhere may experience the love for one another which we share. Praised be Thou, O Lord our G-d, for enabling us to be together on this joyful festival. AMEN.

<u>THIRD NIGHT – STUDY OF TORAH</u>

<u>OPENING PRAYER</u>…On this third night of Chanukah, we rededicate ourselves to the study of our faith and tradition. As the Maccabees courageously fought to preserve our faith, we too are duty-bound to sustain our heritage by deepening our understanding of it through study. By increasing our knowledge of Judaism, we become more sensitive to its abiding values and more aware of our responsibility to realize these values in our society. Study opens our minds and fortifies us against tyranny. Learning secures our freedom. Let us, then, as we kindle these candles, rededicate ourselves to the study of our tradition.

LIGHT SHAMASH, RECITE BLESSINGS, LIGHT CANDLE

Baruch ata Adonai elohaynu melech ha-olam, asher kid'sha-nu b'mitz-vo-tav vitzi-vanu l'hadlik ner shel Chanukah. (Blessed are you, O Lord our G-d, Ruling Spirit of the Universe, who has sanctified us with His commandments, and has commanded us to kindle the Chanukah lights). "We kindle these lights to commemorate the miracles, wonders, triumphs, and victories which You performed through Your holy priests for our ancestors in those days, in this season. These lights are sacred for all eight days of Chanukah. It is forbidden to make any use of them except to look at them in order to praise Your miracles, wonders and triumphs."

Baruch ata Adonai elohaynu melech ha-olam, she'asa ni'sim lo'avotaynu ba'yamim ha'hem baz'man hazeh. (Blessed are you, O Lord our G-d, Ruling spirit of the Universe who has inspired the heroic deeds of our ancestors in times past at this season).

— Take turns around the table with each person talking about what Study of Torah means to them.

— Gifts are exchanged

Biblical passage for THIRD NIGHT (select a reader)

They have eyes, but cannot see; ears, but cannot hear. They are rebels against the light; they are strangers to its ways, and do not stay in its path. For darkness is morning to all of them; for they are friends with the terrors of darkness. Indeed, the light of the wicked fails; the flame of his fire does not shine. The light in his tent darkens; his lamp fails him. They grope without light in the darkness; He makes them wander as if drunk. And I will banish them from the sound of mirth and gladness, the voice of the lamp. All the lights that shine in the sky I will darken above you; and I will bring darkness upon your land – declares the Lord G-d. Listen, you who are deaf; you blind ones; look up and see (Psalms 115:5-6; Job 24:13, 17; Job 18:5-6; 12:25; Jer. 25:10; Ezek. 32:8; Isa. 42:18).

<u>CLOSING PRAYER</u>…O Lord, may we ever recognize our obligation to learn. Increase in us the desire to pursue knowledge as an instrument which strengthens our way of life. Humbly we realize how little we know of our world and our faith. Let those Chanukah lights serve to remind us of our need to study and to increase our understanding. May they inspire us to enlighten and use our minds for the benefit of all people. AMEN.

FOURTH NIGHT – HOPE

<u>OPENING PRAYER</u>…Our ancestors have taught us that in hope everyone's future is illuminated and made creative. Ours are times when many people live in fear and great despair. Like the Maccabees we need to build our lives on hope. Hope that ultimately truth will triumph over falsehood, and confidence that knowledge and understanding will finally depose superstition and tyranny. Now as we kindle these Chanukah lights, may our lives be strengthened by the highest hopes and visions of our faith.

LIGHT SHAMASH, RECITE BLESSINGS, LIGHT CANDLE

Baruch ata Adonai elohaynu melech ha-olam, asher kid'sha-nu b'mitz-vo-tav vitzi-vanu l'hadlik ner shel Chanukah. (Blessed are you, O Lord our G-d, Ruling Spirit of the Universe, who has sanctified us with His commandments, and has commanded us to kindle the Chanukah lights). "We kindle these lights to commemorate the miracles, wonders, triumphs, and victories which You performed through Your holy priests for our ancestors in those days, in this season. These lights are sacred for all eight days of Chanukah. It is forbidden to make any use of them except to look at them in order to praise Your miracles, wonders and triumphs."

Baruch ata Adonai elohaynu melech ha-olam, she'asa ni'sim lo'avotaynu ba'yamim ha'hem baz'man hazeh. (Blessed are you, O Lord our G-d, Ruling spirit of the Universe who has inspired the heroic deeds of our ancestors in times past at this season).

— Take turns around the table with each person talking about what
— Hope means to them.
— Gifts are exchanged

Biblical passage for FOURTH NIGHT (select a reader)

Thus said G-d the Lord, who created the heavens and stretched them out, who spread out the earth and what it brings forth, who gave breath to the people upon it and life to those who walk thereon: I the Lord, in My grace, have summoned you, and I have taken you by the hand. I created you, and appointed you a covenant-people, a light to the nations – Opening eyes deprived of light, rescuing prisoners from confinement, from the dungeon those who sit in the darkness. I form light and create darkness; I make peace and create woe – I the Lord do all these things. I will lead the blind by a road they did not know, and I will make them walk by paths they never knew. I will turn darkness before them into light, rough places into level ground. These are the promises - I will keep them without fail (Isa. 42:5-7; 45:7; 42:16)

CLOSING PRAYER…Eternal our G-d, Source of man's upward striving, inspire us with hope to face courageously the trials and challenges which confront us. Founded upon truth and honesty, may our efforts bring the fulfillment of our highest aspirations. We sincerely hope for the day when all people will be free, when war will no longer delay the dawn of justice and peace. Praised art Thou, O Lord, who encourages our desire for a better tomorrow and our steadfast hope in the future. AMEN.

FIFTH NIGHT – TZEDAKAH

<u>OPENING PRAYER</u>…Our tradition tells us that during the Maccabean war for freedom, all Jews, both children and adults, contributed tzedakah toward the cause of defeating the oppressor. There are many forms of oppression still existent in our world today. There are people afflicted by sickness, hunger, ignorance, and prejudice. Tonight, we like our ancestors, put aside gifts of tzedakah in order that we too may help bring an end to oppression. We pray that the humble gifts we offer will provide food for the hungry, medicine for the sick, knowledge for the ignorant, and equal opportunity for those afflicted by prejudice (Each member of the family can now tell what his/her gift of tzedakah will be.)

LIGHT SHAMASH, RECITE BLESSINGS, LIGHT CANDLE

Baruch ata Adonai elohaynu melech ha-olam, asher kid'sha-nu b'mitz-vo-tav vitzi-vanu l'hadlik ner shel Chanukah. (Blessed are you, O Lord our G-d, Ruling Spirit of the Universe, who has sanctified us with His commandments, and has commanded us to kindle the Chanukah lights). "We kindle these lights to commemorate the miracles, wonders, triumphs, and victories which You performed through Your holy priests for our ancestors in those days, in this season. These lights are sacred for all eight days of Chanukah. It is forbidden to make any use of them except to look at them in order to praise Your miracles, wonders and triumphs."

Baruch ata Adonai elohaynu melech ha-olam, she'asa ni'sim lo'avotaynu ba'yamim ha'hem baz'man hazeh. (Blessed are you, O Lord our G-d, Ruling spirit of the Universe who has inspired the heroic deeds of our ancestors in times past at this season).

— Take turns around the table with each person talking about what Tzedakah means to them.
— Gifts are exchanged

Biblical passage for FIFTH NIGHT (select a reader)

Look at me, answer me, O Lord, my G-d! Give light to my eyes lest I sleep the sleep of death. Darkness is not dark for you; night is as light as day; darkness and light are the same. Now therefore, O our G-d, listen to the prayer of your servant, and to his supplications, and cause Your face to shine upon Your sanctuary that is desolate, for the Lord's sake. Send forth Your light and Your truth; they will lead me; they will bring me to Your holy mountain, to your dwelling-place. With You is the fountain of life; by Your light do we see light. It is You who light my lamp; the Lord, my G-d, light up my darkness. The soul of a human is the lamp of the Lord, searching all the innermost parts. For You have saved me from death, my foot from stumbling, that I may walk before G-d in the light of my life. Truly, G-d does all these things, two, three times to a person, to bring him back from the Pit, that he may bask in the light of life (Ps. 13:4; 139:12; Dan. 9:17; Ps. 43:3; 36:10; 18:29; Prov. 20:27; Ps. 56:14; Job. 33: 29-30)

CLOSING PRAYER…Our G-d and G-d of our fathers, we have been taught that the more tzedakah there is, the more secure does peace become. May our Chanukah candles symbolize for us the light of happiness and hope which our tzedakah will bring to those oppressed by need. Aid us, O Lord, to be compassionate and generous toward our people. Praised be thou, O Lord, who inspires within us the will to do tzedakah, and a concern for the welfare and dignity of all people. AMEN.

SIXTH NIGHT – PEACE

OPENING PRAYER…The candles of Chanukah remind us of our chosen mission as Jews. Like the Maccabees, we seek to rededicate ourselves to the service of G-d. Today, one of our foremost tasks is to secure peace in our troubled world. When we end disagreements through mutual understandings, when we seek to mend hurt and wounded feelings, we are doing our part in making peace a living ideal. Let us, as we kindle our Chanukah candles, rededicate ourselves with renewed strength to the task of securing peace.

LIGHT SHAMASH, RECITE BLESSINGS, LIGHT CANDLE

Baruch ata Adonai elohaynu melech ha-olam, asher kid'sha-nu b'mitz-vo-tav vitzi-vanu l'hadlik ner shel Chanukah. (Blessed are you, O Lord our G-d, Ruling Spirit of the Universe, who has sanctified us with His commandments, and has commanded us to kindle the Chanukah lights). "We kindle these lights to commemorate the miracles, wonders, triumphs, and victories which You performed through Your holy priests for our ancestors in those days, in this season. These lights are sacred for all eight days of Chanukah. It is forbidden to make any use of them except to look at them in order to praise Your miracles, wonders and triumphs."

Baruch ata Adonai elohaynu melech ha-olam, she'asa ni'sim lo'avotaynu ba'yamim ha'hem baz'man hazeh. (Blessed are you, O Lord our G-d, Ruling spirit of the Universe who has inspired the heroic deeds of our ancestors in times past at this season).

— Take turns around the table with each person talking about what Peace means to them.

— Gifts are exchanged

Biblical passage for SIXTH NIGHT (select a reader)

The Lord is my light and my help whom shall I fear? Bless the Lord, O my soul; O Lord, my G-d. You are very great; You are clothed in glory and majesty, wrapped in a robe of light; You spread the heavens like a tent cloth. Your world is a lamp to my feet, a light for my path. The precepts of the Lord are just, rejoicing in His heart, the instruction of the Lord is lucid, giving light to my eyes. For the commandment is a lamp, and the Torah is a light. Enlighten our eyes in Your Torah, attach our heart to Your commandments, unite our heart to love and revere Your name. (Ps. 27:1; 104:1-2; 119-105; 19-9; Prov. 6-23; traditional prayer book).

CLOSING PRAYER…O Lord, our G-d, show the pathway of peace to all. Teach us that the only acts which flow out of kinship and goodwill can bring enduring peace. Help us to realize that hate and prejudice bring nothing but strife and chaos into the world. Let all people recognize that only through cooperation and honest negotiation can the inhabitants of the earth be strengthened. Praised be Thou, O Lord, Giver of Peace.

SEVENTH NIGHT – COMMUNITY

OPENING PRAYER…Community is founded upon a total respect for the liberty and freedom of all people. The Maccabees of old sought to protect themselves when their rights were violated. Our Chanukah lights serve as a reminder that community is secure only when we honor the precious liberty and property of our people.

As we kindle these lights, let us rededicate ourselves to the cause of community which alone can bring dignity to all people.

LIGHT SHAMASH, RECITE BLESSINGS, LIGHT CANDLE

Baruch ata Adonai elohaynu melech ha-olam, asher kid'sha-nu b'mitz-vo-tav vitzi-vanu l'hadlik ner shel Chanukah. (Blessed are you, O Lord our G-d, Ruling Spirit of the Universe, who has sanctified us with His commandments, and has commanded us to kindle the Chanukah lights). "We kindle these lights to commemorate the miracles, wonders, triumphs, and victories which You performed through Your holy priests for our ancestors in those days, in this season. These lights are sacred for all eight days of Chanukah. It is forbidden to make any use of them except to look at them in order to praise Your miracles, wonders and triumphs." Baruch ata Adonai elohaynu melech ha-olam, she'asa ni'sim lo'avotaynu ba'yamim ha'hem baz'man hazeh. (Blessed are you, O Lord our G-d, Ruling spirit of the Universe who has inspired the heroic deeds of our ancestors in times past at this season).

— Take turns around the table with each person talking about what Community means to them.
— Gifts are exchanged

Biblical passage for SEVENTH NIGHT (select a reader)

For the path of the righteous is as the light of dawn, that shines brighter and brighter until full day. Light is sown for the righteous, radiance for the upright. O you righteous, rejoice in the Lord and acclaim His holy name. The people that walked in darkness have seen a brilliant light; on those who dwelt in a land of gloom light has dawned. For all the Israelites enjoyed light in their dwellings. Arise, shine, for your light has dawned; the Presence of the Lord has shone upon you! O House of Jacob! Come, let us walk by the light of the Lord. (Prov. 4:18; Ps. 97:11-12; Isa. 9:1; Exod. 10:23; Isa. 60:1; 2:5).

CLOSING PRAYER...Our G-d, teach us to be sensitive to the feelings of our friends and neighbors. Help us to understand their failings and grant us the humility to praise and applaud their achievements. May our Chanukah candles remind us that all people are created equal in Thy sight. Praised be Thou, O Lord, who would have every human being cherish the community and unity of all peoples. AMEN.

EIGHTH NIGHT – FAITH

OPENING PRAYER...Tonight we kindle all the candles of our Chanukah Menorah. Throughout the centuries the menorah has been a symbol of our faith, Judaism. Like the Maccabees, when they celebrated this festive holiday, we rededicate ourselves to the living of a more meaningful Jewish life. We pray that throughout this coming year we may fulfill the ideals of freedom, tzedakah, family, study, hope, peace, and community, all of which are symbolized by the candles of our menorah.

LIGHT SHAMASH, RECITE BLESSINGS, LIGHT CANDLE

Baruch ata Adonai elohaynu melech ha-olam, asher kid'sha-nu b'mitz-vo-tav vitzi-vanu l'hadlik ner shel Chanukah. (Blessed are you, O Lord our G-d, Ruling Spirit of the Universe, who has sanctified us with His commandments, and has commanded us to kindle the Chanukah lights). "We kindle these lights to commemorate the miracles, wonders, triumphs, and victories which You performed through Your holy priests for our ancestors in those days, in this season. These lights are sacred for all eight days of Chanukah. It is forbidden to make any use of them except to look at them in order to praise Your miracles, wonders and triumphs."

Baruch ata Adonai elohaynu melech ha-olam, she'asa ni'sim lo'avotaynu ba'yamim ha'hem baz'man hazeh. (Blessed are you, O Lord our G-d, Ruling spirit of the Universe who has inspired the heroic deeds of our ancestors in times past at this season).

— Take turns around the table with each person talking about what Faith means to them.
— Gifts are exchanged

Biblical passage for EIGHTH NIGHT (select a reader)

Behold, there will come a time! And the light of the moon shall become like the light of the sun, and the light of the sun shall become sevenfold, like the light of the seven days, when the lord binds up His people's wounds and heals the injuries it has suffered. In that day, there shall be neither sunlight nor cold moonlight but there shall be a continuous day, of neither day nor night, and there shall be light at evening time. No longer shall you need the sun for light by day nor the shining of the moon for radiance by night; for the Lord shall be your light everlasting, your G-d shall be your glory. Your sun shall set no more, your moon no more withdraw; for the Lord shall be a light to you forever. Cause a new light to shine upon Zion and soon may all of us be worthy to enjoy its light (Isa. 30:26; Zech 14:6-7; Isa, 60:19-20; traditional prayer book).

Note: During the last night, I read the book of Judith in dedication to my wife and summarize it for the family. http://www.eskimo. com/~lhowell/bcp1662/apocrypha/judith.html

CLOSING PRAYER...Our G-d and G-d of our fathers, may we be sustained and strengthened by our faith. Through our study of it and through our devotion to its ideals, we pray that we shall speed the day when all people will recognize that they are brothers and sisters. Then will Thy kingdom be established, and peace on earth be made secure. Praised be Thou O Lord for the faith of our ancestors, and or the opportunity of celebrating our holiday of Chanukah. AMEN.

Closing thoughts

I arrived in Kuwait and Iraq during Chanukah. Lisa and I met during the end of Chanukah and one of our first family observances was Chanukah. We love the themes for each night because they give us something to do and to discuss around the table.

CHAPTER EIGHT

Adult Bar Mitzvah

*A*pril 17, 2009, was the day that I became Bar Mitzvah. Reaching this milestone in my Jewish Journey was never a doubt. It was only a matter of when. At most synagogues Adult Bar Mitzvah classes are held. The class can take 6 months to a year to complete. The curriculum includes but is not limited to Hebrew lessons, studying Torah, learning the particular Torah portion, developing the D'var Torah, coming up with a theme, leading a service, chanting Torah and coming up with a Mitzvah project. I loved every minute of it. Rabbi asked me to be the group leader and manage the final outcome.

The Torah section was Tazria Metzora. A rather difficult section to get your arms around because it deals with blisters, boils and basic diseases of the skin. I recall spending many hours with my Dad, Michael, going over the blessings, reading from the Torah which can be tricky for those not familiar with Hebrew. Chanting our Torah portion was challenging but fun. Rabbi provided the group with theirsection on CD. I took it to the next level by recording it on my phone and playing it wherever I went. When it came time for the actual ceremony, I am fairly certain that my family could have chanted my portion without even reading it.

For me, the experience cemented my dedication and sense of resolve at being Jewish. Our faith demands action in just about every encounter with ordinary daily activities. It begins with reciting the Modeh Ani before getting out of bed in the morning and continues throughout the day with blessing food, reciting the Amidah 3 times a day, saying a prayer upon departure and entry into any dwelling and of course repeating the Shema as many times as possible. I find myself praying throughout the day for little miracles that I encounter along my daily route.

As an adult going through a Bar Mitzvah instead of being 13 years old, I understand what it took to get to this point. Making a decision to complete this level of my education was so much more than a rite of passage; it was part of the life-long commitment to being Jewish. The experience taught me a deeper understanding of conducting services, history of our people, the meaning behind our prayers, a closer look at the Mishnah and the meaning behind many of our rituals. Being a Bar Mitzvah was tantamount to completing another layer of understanding and belief. I am a part of all who have come before me. A spiritual awakening took place on that day at Temple Sinai on the Bima. It's hard to put my finger on it, but every week when I enter Shul and recite the prayer upon entering the sanctuary, I have such an intense feeling of connectedness that I often feel myself choking back the tears.

<u>Julian's D'var Torah Speech: Military perspective</u>

Our Torah portion is "Tazria" and the condition is not an ordinary, physical disease; rather, it is a divinely sent punishment that one may suffer in retribution for specific improprieties. Tzaraas, according to the Torah is an outward expression of an inner spiritual ailment.

In an effort to link the Torah portion to my preparation for this moment, an outward expression of an inner spiritual ailment, I will share with you the story of how I arrived at this moment and the emotions that I experienced and overcame.

The transition to greater responsibility and becoming an adult began when I graduated from High School, joined the Merchant Marines and experienced my first Bar Mitzvah ceremony as a guest while in Haifa, Israel in 1979. My curiosity and research into Judaism continued when I entered the Navy in 1980 and grew over the next 30 years. I have been fortunate enough to visit Israel two additional times while serving in the Navy. I can vividly recall praying at the "wailing wall" and encountering the presence and meaning of Jewish life during those visits. Talmudic privileges bestow upon a person that has completed his or her Bar/Bat Mitzvah as being counted as part of a minyan, offering testimony and making vows. The zeitgeist spanning the past 49 years has culminated in this single event today.

At the onset, when I learned of the Adult Bar Mitzvah class I was in awe, excited, happy, aggressive (wanting to get started right away) and somewhat fearful of the daunting task that lay ahead. I am a perfectionist by nature, and as such, the anticipation of requirements left me a bit uneasy. I knew the Hebrew alphabet, but I had not mastered it.

The inner turmoil manifested itself in outward expressions or manifestations of insomnia and cycles of increased anxiety towards the upcoming class (2-x per month) because I was not as prepared as I needed to be. I had to formulate an attack, like preparing for a military assignment.

Lynn would probably say that I was on edge and with my note cards always in tow, I read, chanted and rehearsed several times a day over the span of 6 months or so. My plan was executed in two phases. Phase 1 was solicitation of a tutor and involved Mr. Michael and Mrs. Lucy Sukman, my adopted parents. Mike and I met routinely from day one, several times per week. We studied blessings, my Torah portion and Mike sent numerous audio files to me, so that I could hear and pronounce the course materials properly.

When audio files could not be found, Mike called my phone and read the Torah portions on my voice mail for me to listen to on my own. When I experienced car trouble, on one occasion, we studied in his vehicle as we drove to Gloucester. Our meeting places included Shul, his home, Panera's and Starbucks. Phase 2 was practice, practice, practice. My system involved morning chanting in the shower and reading my portions every evening before bed and at lunch time as part of my daily prayers. Collectively my internal emotions that finally clicked included: joy, affection, enthrallment, cheerfulness, enthusiasm, contentment, triumph, pride, relief, optimism and zest. The outward manifestation of the emotions is the finished product that you see today.

The sine qua non of my journey without question was my assignment to Iraq on a 436 day tour to Baghdad where I served as the second Jewish Lay Leader for the International Zone. It was during that tour that I held services in Sadaam Hussein's palace, experienced a complete year of high holidays and shared experiences with Jews from all occupations and walks of life that included the State Department, Blackwater, Contractors, all Armed Services, local Iraqi Jews, and the wonderful support from local and international Jewish agencies. I can still recall scheduling and planning covert operations every Shabbat service for one of the Iraqi Jews, one of seven that remained in Baghdad, where she could not worship freely because of persecution.

Two of us, on a rotational basis, would mount an armored HUMV, weapons loaded, body armor affixed and would meet and escort our fellow Jew through the numerous check points, just to ensure that Khalida could worship with family. The situation re-instilled within me, the significance of attending services and the fact that she was willing to risk her life just to experience Shabbat. I would be remiss if I did not mention my fallen comrade, Major Stuart Adam Wolfer, blessed be his name, with whom, was fatally wounded on April 6th, 2008, during a mortar attack on the compound where we worked together. Stuart was going to be the next Lay Leader of B'nai Baghdad. He was a friend, a brother, a workout partner, a soldier in arms, a Father, Husband, Son and a fellow Jew. I still remember the 6 of us rushing to the morgue when we heard of his death, being escorted to see him, and reciting psalms until the Angel flight came to take him away from us. As a Shomrim, we honored him and never left him alone. The strength of Major Elizabeth Robbins in coordinating everything was awe inspiring.

This journey, this moment as described by one of my favorite blessings, Shehekianu, has been long, arduous and often times met with incredible amounts of uncertainty and stress. On July 8, 2010, my 50th Birthday, I will retire from the United States Navy, completing 30 years of uninterrupted service.

I have no doubt in my mind that it was because of my service that I am a proud and devout Jew. But know this, as sure as I am standing here today, I owe a debt of gratitude to Jodie Leah Lynn and beautiful children, Rabbi Scott Gurdin, Temple Sinai family, B'nai Baghdad Family, Mike and Lucy Sukman, My Mom and all the prayers from friends, that acted as a shield to allow me to reach this hallowed day where I am finally able to have a Bar Mitzvah! Today is not the end of the journey and transition, it is the beginning. Thank you.

An example of one of many emails to the Adult Bar Mitzvah Group that I was privileged and honored to lead. All correspondence to the group was copied to our Rabbi.

From: Wyatt, Julian C. LCDR <3mo@cvn77.navy.mil>
To: Adult Bar Mitzvah Study Group
Date: Fri, Apr 2, 2010, at 6:02 PM
Subject: D'var Torah Feedback – speech length and common theme

Good Evening Everyone,

Here is what I have so far on the D'var Torah Speech length:

   Jules: 5 minutes (Iraq & Military perspective)

   Lona: 5 minutes (Diversity)

   Paul: 5 minutes (Mikvah and family)

   Rebecca: 2 minutes (Shabbat service at the fire circle)

   Megan: in progress

If Megan's D'var Torah length is between 2-5 minutes (5 minutes being max), then we are at 22 minutes for our collective speech. My goal is no more than 15 minutes total for everyone. Rebecca's D'var Torah is right on the mark. Super job Rebecca!! My research on the D'var Torah has resulted in the following goal or purpose statement for the speech:

"A brief explanation of the meaning of a Bar/Bat Mitzvah, event or an essay by the Bar/Bat Mitzvah on the meaning of the day to him/her." I consider brief to be 2-3 minutes and I intend to edit mine to meet that objective. I am asking for your assistance to consolidate your remarks to fit that objective. In reading the individual heartfelt speeches, I was moved and touched by what this special day means to each one of you. Thank you for including me and for sending it to me.

The original intent is to adopt a common theme as a group so that when the introduction of our theme is read, each person that stands up is telling part of our story, instead of 5 completely, separate and distinct stories. I don't get the sense that we have a common theme and that each one of our stories ties into that common theme. If you look at what I surmise to be your main point, you will see that we are extremely diverse which is not a bad thing, but as I understood Rabbi's direction, one central theme relating to Tazria or something else agreed upon, should be the goal.

I like the fact that we span several generational gaps – from the Silent Generation (born between 1930 and 1945); Baby Boomer generation (born between 1946 and 1964); through Generation X (also known as baby busters born between 1965 and 1977) and ultimately to Generation Y (born between 1977 and 1997). As Paul so eloquently put it in his speech "Passing the Torah between the generations is a central part of our spiritual existence and it is indeed an honor to share this moment." Perhaps we can weave this into our common theme a little better?

For this collective, iterative speech to tell a story, I need your help, or rather suggestions. If I had my druthers, it would have been so much easier to assign parts like our script for the service, where each person speaks about "one" mutually agreed upon element that fits into "our" collective story. Does this make sense at all?

I'm scratching my head on this one and would like if at all possible, to get together with the group at Shul between noon and 2pm on March 12th and March 13th. Is this at all possible? Again, great job on this one, I just think we need to edit a few things out and try and establish a common theme where everyone adds to the collective theme in their personal story, each person building upon what the previous person just spoke about. I hope this makes sense.

Oh...one more thing, I have all but one speech and if you agree, I will send out all of them to the entire group – but I need your permission or rather disclosure agreement to make sure that you are okay with me sharing what you wrote and sent to me and Rabbi, with the entire group.

Shabbat shalom, Netzach ShebeChesed – Today is four days of the Omer. My best to your families!!!

Jules

Closing thoughts

Adult Bar and Bat Mitzvah versus having a Bar and Bat Mitzvah as a child (12 and 13 years old)? If you have ever considered experiencing this life cycle event and you are on the fence about going through the process as an adult, please don't be! I learned so much about my faith, my knowledge, the Torah, our traditions and customs, in addition to reading the Torah, that I will never, everforget.

In particular, as a Jew-by-Choice, you already made the commitment and you've taken all steps to convert. You have alreadyanswered the "why" because of your decision. It is my personal opinion that the experience of having a Bar/Bat Mitzvah as an adult, is epic in your continued study of Judaism. The experience was very spiritual and emotional for me. A deeper connection was forgedwith my Bar Mitzvah and it will be for you as well.

CHAPTER NINE

Correspondence from the front lines

The following are copies of various emails during my 436 day deployment to Iraq. My Mom wrote me a letter a day, for 436 days straight. She is amazing! Lovingly, Mr. Wonderful (her nickname for me).

The email that saved my life:

-----Original Message-----
From: Page, Robert LTJG MNSTC-I J4
Sent: Sunday, April 06, 2008, 12:37 PM
To: Wyatt, Julian LCDR MNSTC-I DDA
Subject: gym at 1300 vice 1315?
Can you go at 1300?
V/R
Bobby
Robert L. Page, LTJG, USN
MNSTC-I J-4/Ammunition Section OIC

-----Original Message-----
From: Wyatt, Julian LCDR MNSTC-I DDA
Sent: Sunday, April 06, 2008, 12:37 PM

To: Page, Robert LTJG MNSTC-I J4

Subject: RE: gym at 1300 vice 1315?

Sir. Yes, Sir.

Very respectfully,

Jules

Julian C. Wyatt, LCDR, LDO, USN

MNSTC-I, DDA, Sustainment FCT

-----Original Message-----

From: Page, Robert LTJG MNSTC-I J4

Sent: Sunday, April 06, 2008, 4:47 PM

To: Wyatt, Julian LCDR MNSTC-I DDA

Cc: Bachand, Peter CDR MNSTC-I DDA

Subject: RE: gym at 1300 vice 1315?

Jules,

I guess the time change was a good idea huh? We are good to go Bro.

V/R

Bobby

-----Original Message-----

From: Wyatt, Julian LCDR MNSTC-I DDA

Sent: Sunday, April 06, 2008, 4:49 PM

To: Page, Robert LTJG MNSTC-I J4

Cc: Bachand, Peter CDR MNSTC-I DDA

Subject: RE: gym at 1300 vice 1315?

I just thought about that....If we had started our workout at 1315, we would have been in the gym at the time of the attack. You saved our life bro....That is very scary.

I love you man ☺

Jules

<u>Letter to Mom</u>

From: Julian Wyatt

Date: Sat, Oct 20, 2007, at 5:19 PM

Subject: Please read this Letter to Mom – thank you

My Dearest Heart,

A lifetime has passed since we sat together, back to back, in the living room in New Jersey, one by one, listening, speaking and feeling the energy emanate from one another – a hallowed sacred circle of trust, freedom, and oneness of self-expression. I have traveled thousands of miles since that brief and life altering ritual Mom; and I have also had the privilege to love and be loved, each time, subconsciously and consciously equating that person, to the relationship that we developed so many years prior and continue to this day.

Everything I have done, everyone I have encountered on this endless journey, in some way comes back to you, full circle; the beginning of my existence and your careful, methodical coaching, mentoring, and cultivation of seeds of greatness – that have taken root within the chambers of my heart and now...will continue to echo throughout eternity. I can find no gift more significant and truly representative of how much my heart and others have been touched, merely by having had the opportunity and privilege to know you and receive your love, than a Levian, Chocolate Diamond Heart Pendant.

The heart in the center is and has always been my love for you – all encompassing, radiating outwards, touching, moving, and gracing everyone within its path. Please take a look at all those shiny diamond chips in its core and on the outer borders – those are family, friends, strangers, adopted daughters and sons – some military and some civilian. Their star now shines so much brighter all because of you. We continue to carry you within our hearts, keeping you alive wherever we go and whatever we do, a loving and gentle compass, nudging us back to true north, with a gentle whisper rustling in the tress and riding in the wind: "you can do anything you put your mind to and don't forget to help others whenever you can, I love you honey." Thank you.

On behalf of the thousands of people you have touched and continue to love, Lynn and I represent them as messengers – thanking you on behalf of them, with this heart.

Please know that regardless of where you are, what you are doing, the trials and tribulations you are facing and will continue to face in the long days and nights ahead, we are standing watch over you, so that you no longer have to worry, no longer have to despair...we will worry and despair for you my love.

Happy belated birthday, happy belated Mothers' Day!

With all that I am, with all that I will ever be,
I send to you this day and every day,
My enduring love, appreciation, gratitude and
most passionate and tender embrace.
I remain, always –
Mr. Wonderful

<u>To Lynn:</u>

Thank you for everything, which includes my conversion to Judaism. "You made that happen" and I am eternally grateful to you! This tour was arduous enough and you made it easier by the daily emails to me and the bi-monthly emails to my command. Additionally, routine phone calls, care packages and of course, keeping me calm amongst all the chaos was exceptional. I know at times things were rough (my issues) and yet you never let it come between us. My first counseling session upon return to the States due to insomnia, night sweats and mood irregularity was so very helpful. Lastly, your help with establishing a website for B'nai Baghdad in honor of Stuart, was simply amazing. Thank you for keeping me supplied with cigars (smile). I appreciate you friend. Love, Jewels

<u>Electronic Letter of Appreciation – Unsung heroes</u>

Wyatt, Julian LCDR MNSTC-I DDA <julian.wyatt@iraq.centcom.mil>
To: Friends and Family E-mail group
Date: Tue, Oct 28, 2008, at 3:13 AM
Subject: Electronic Letter of Appreciation – Unsung heroes
Tuesday, October 28, 2008

Baghdad, Iraq – Last day
12:16 p.m. –

Dearest Family,

As my tour of 436 days finally creeps to an end, I would be remiss if I did not personally thank all of you for your love and support during such an arduous tour of duty in Iraq. I could not have accomplished as much, if it were not for your love, your prayers, the e-mails, the almost daily letters (Mom), care packages, constant encouragement and phone calls (Lynn).

You are the "Unsung Heroes" that deserve medals, accolades, a standing ovation and personal recognition. I was successful during this tour, only because you were right here beside me, surrounding me, letting me know, that I was never alone. I felt it. During every mortar attack, as I huddled in the duck and cover cement cave, body armor and helmet securely in place, while round after round hit Phoenix Base where I work and Blackhawk compound where I laid half awake, poised ready for the next alarm...and the constant wailing of helicopters, carrying the soldiers, some wounded, to the local hospital and others, home to their loved ones, in a peaceful sleep...I always felt a presence, that I was not alone, despite so much anxiety, the unknown, feelings of loneliness and being separated.

It is difficult at best to put into words, the uncertainty of war and pending death. Never knowing what to expect; whether on a bus going to or coming from work transiting around the Green Zone; eating in the chow hall; working out in the gym; sleeping; or on my way to worship – if today is the day. My faith was a fulcrum point in allowing me to feel loved and to know that I was not alone. I found comfort in that understanding. Not once, did I ever take one day for granted.

I suppose this is a myopic view, from the soldier's perspective. However, as I shift the focal lens to embrace all of you, at home, watching the news, waiting to hear from me, to know that I survived the last volley of attacks that are being broadcasted, and yet, having to keep your wits about you, for the children, for family, for colleagues, for well-wishers and supporters of this noble cause...maintaining your emotional state, could not have been easy. Physically you may not have been right here in the battlefield, but in every other perspective, I can relate to the range and depth of the scale of emotions that you must have been going through. I echo that spectrum and I want you to know I never lost sight of it. War takes its toll on everyone.

As many of you are aware, I lost one close colleague, Colonel Scott and one brother, Major Stuart Wolfer, during this tour. I stood over them in the hospital, prayed over Stuart, surrounding him in love and comfort as the tears blanketed my desert uniform. Death has a way of changing you, nothing is ever the same again. I grew stronger in my faith as a result. Another family that I would have never known, adopted me and I them, (Mom Ester and Sister Beverly) and a quiet peace enveloped me. I resolved to live each day fully and completely – with passion, with love and with a sense of growing inner peace and strength.

I have learned a lot from this tour, the way of life of a soldier, living in trailers, walking to take showers, living in my body armor, eating rations, traveling in HUMV's, taking helicopter rides as a safer mode of transportation, and developing working relationships with local Iraqi Nationals, that brave everything, just for a better way of life. But, most importantly, I learned the value of family and how important it is to feel loved and a part of the everyday life, back at home. I always felt connected. To me, this was my lifeline and panacea for loneliness, depression, insomnia, hyper alertness, etc. I owe that to all of you above. I just don't have the words to adequately convey how much you were instrumental in my success as an American Soldier. Without you, every one of you, I could not, would not, have made it through this tour.

<u>To Mom,</u>

With the exception of a few tardy mail calls, I received a letter each day, with love, encouragement, notes, cartoons and the atmosphere that only you can impart. I remember everything you have taught me and I tried my best to honor you and our family name. Thank you for the gift of life. I love you and I miss you.

<u>To Mom Esther,</u>

Thank you for the gift of your son and my brother Stuart. I am a better man having had the pleasure of knowing him and working with him. I am bringing home his love to you and a long overdue hug.

Two days ago, I received a Bronze Star. The award was pinned on my uniform by a British Brigadier General, Johnny Torrens-Spence. All I could think about was Stuart during the award presentation -adjacent to the Phoenix Base Gym. I have since acquired a second Bronze Star (not earned, I just wanted two medals to bring back with me). Upon my return and when we meet, one is for you (the one that was pinned on my Uniform) and the other is for Beverly. It is what Stuart would have wanted – his brother to bring home the medal that he also earned and hand deliver it to Mom and his Sister. I love you, Hillel.

To Nik,

I will miss our rendezvous at the Victory Base launch pad and Stryker Stables and catching the midnight Rhino. I am so relieved to know that you are departing Iraq early. I can't wait for you to be back home, safe and sound. I love you, Daddy

To my children and grandchildren,

I miss you so very much. Thank you for the beautiful drawings of me in uniform (smile), your love and prayers, the marathon conversation Dan, and for continuing to be the best that you can be, every day. I can't wait to see you and to hold you in my arms. I love you.

To my Sisters, Brothers, Nephew, etc.,

Thank you for the frequent and constant check-ins...and when I did not respond, the more direct and frequent check-ins (smile). To my brothers I came to love and rediscover in Iraq, words can't even begin to describe how you have assisted me in this tour. Thank you Kelly and Rich. To Dee...thank you for being such a prince to Lynn, during Rick's illness.

You gave her strength, support, love and assistance, all of which I could not physically do. You are amazing. I love you and thank you Dee.

Sister Beverly, albeit we have not physically met, we are connected on a spiritual level and I can't wait to finally meet you. Today I read "On Flanders Field's" and took photos of the gym, the last place where Stuart drew breath. A short video clip was also recorded of this moment. Thank you for all that you have given to me during this tour. Love, Hillel

<u>To CDR Pete Bachand.,</u>

I cannot imagine how I would have survived this tour, to include training at Fort Riley, without your guidance, leadership, brotherly love, support, and humor. We survived it! Thank you for all the mentorship over our overlapping tours of duty. You always fought for me and I will never forget it brother. Love, Jules

Julian H.C. Wyatt, LCDR, LDO, USN, MNSTC-I, DDA Logistics Assistant Munitions Management Officer, "AMMO"
Phoenix Base APO AE 09348

<u>To CDR Glen Bourque.,</u>

Shitty (our nickname for each other), we met during our first tour of duty after book camp, the USS Sterett (CG-31) in 1980 and our bond has only grown through the years to include being my first born's (Diana) GodFather, you were there in Subic Bay, Republic of the Philippines. Thank you for taking care of the family while I was deployed to Iraq my brother and for allowing me to vent whenever I needed to. You still do. I appreciate you and I love you. Thank you for being my best friend.

Closing thoughts

I wish I opened up and shared more of what I was feeling about the experience of being in Iraq and the changes that I was undergoing with my colleagues. In particular, after the death of Stuart, I was never the same again and the situation played into my work life, family life and love life, until I sought help.

Lynn and Mom with the identical necklace (2007)

CHAPTER TEN: NOVEMBER 21ST, 2013

Admitting that something is wrong and getting diagnosed

Thursday Morning, November 21st, 2013, I awoke in my home after yet another night of tossing and turning. The dreams consisted mostly of nightmares, dreaming of death, seeing myself in a coffin, memories of bunkers in Iraq, constant shelling, seeing Stuart alive one moment and then dead a few hours later, feeling the heat of Iraq and sweating profusely and struggling to breathe. On this particular morning, I woke up hearing the sounds of helicopters, which remind me of Iraq – they flew constantly over Baghdad.

One thing was different though, I felt at peace. A sense of numbness and disassociation that I have experienced repeatedly since 2008, typically after being extremely angry and then distant. It feels like an out of body experience where I am watching myself all day long, as if hovering with a video camera. I have contemplated suicide on many occasions since Iraq. The need to feel connected, whole, at peace and happy about something, anything.

Lynn left early for work as usual. I got up in a fog. Showered, dressed, ready to go to school to teach and then changed my mind. I went to my dresser, pulled out my gun, grabbed a magazine, inserted it, walked into the bathroom, placed a bunch of towels in the bathtub and then I heard the sound of my grandchildren downstairs with my son and daughter in law! I remembered that they temporarily moved in with us a week ago while waiting to get a new place. I thought about what they would see when they entered the bathroom and I froze. I unloaded the magazine, put the gun back and decided there must be another way and instead of going to work, I would get in my car and drive, to a place of solitude.

As I walked into the living room, my son Daniel was on the couch watching a show on television. He asked me to sit and watch it with him, as if trying to prevent me from leaving. I sat down briefly but felt very uneasy. I wanted to leave. Finally, I gave him a hug, a very deep and passionate hug, kissed his cheek and told him I loved him. I walked out of the house knowing I would never return.

While in the car, I received a phone call from the Mitsubishi Dealer in Glendale, AZ., about an oil dipstick that I ordered because mine cracked and I could not change my oil without it. The guy said come and get it. The drive would take me to Glendale far away from home. Everything was coming together.

I parked my car in the parking lot, feeling such a sense of peace and contentment that I have not felt before. As I walked in the door, a Vietnam Veteran was standing outside smoking a cigarette.

I saw his ball cap. I walked over and shook his hand and said, "Welcome home Brother." He held my hand looking at me or rather through me. He let go after 30 seconds or 1 minute...very uncomfortable amount of time. He said, "How are you doing?" I replied "today I feel at peace, for the first time in a very long time." He started talking about Vietnam and having been diagnosed with PTSD long after the war. He said that he was headed to a group counseling session and if I wanted to attend with him. I explained that I was never diagnosed with PTSD. He said only you know if you are still having difficulty coping with this life, he said, combat changes you forever.

After talking for about 30 minutes or so, he made a call to the VA to find out the name of the clinic where I could get more information on PTSD, it was called the "Jade/Opal Clinic." I thanked him and walked inside to the parts counter. I exited and walked over to my car and lifted the hood. Changed the oil cap and dip stick and when I turned around the parts guy was standing beside me. He actually startled me. He asked if my oil needed to be changed. I replied "yes, but I need to go." At this point I was sweating profusely and my heart was racing." He explained that it was cheaper than any other place and they wash and vacuum the car. It was as if he would not take no for an answer. I said "okay" and returned to the waiting room. My buddy the Vietnam Veteran was still present.

He sat down beside me and asked about my family and tour in Iraq. We spoke a lot about Stuart, seeing him in the body bag, unzipped in the morgue. I talked at length about anger, rage, disappointment in G-d, in myself and feeling sick to my stomach every time I thought about the shelling. I wanted someone to pay for taking his life, for people around me to understand his sacrifice, and the fact that this world was not real. We talked about feeling numb and wanting to die, just letting go. He continued to speak about family and about being changed forever and that it was okay.

I remember putting my head down on the table and crying. Shaking violently. I looked up at one point and he was gone! Poof. Just like that. It was then, that I text messaged Lynn and said I was heading to the VA to check myself in for help. That it was time. She cried on the phone and said I will meet you there.

I sat in the parking lot for ever. Lynn arrived and we walked in together holding hands. She never let go. I was taken to a room. I talked to several people. The Doctor was kind and understanding. He recommended in-patient care. Reluctantly, I agreed and was admitted. No phone. No wallet. No identity beyond my kippot and prayer book. It was the longest 48 hours of my life. I was in a room with 6 other beds. I had green pajamas on, slippers, a white bathrobe and received meds that were dispensed every 6 hours or so at a window. I could not relax due to the "crazies" on the floor.

I spoke to the intake person and learned a lot about myself and this struggle. We talked about fear, suicide, anger and losing people. For the first time, I think I found someone that understood. The Doctors and case worker were phenomenal. I was released to my son, Daniel. He waited for 6 hours in the lobby. He refused to leave without me. I embraced him and we held each other for some time. We went to eat and I think we saw a movie. The day was a blur as I recall.

A week or so later, I made an appointment with the Vet Center in Phoenix and began the process of healing through EMDR (Eye Movement Desensitization and Reprocessing). I feel very close to my Rabbi, Dean Shapiro at Temple Emanuel of Tempe. We had several conversations about death and dying. Rabbi told me in one conversation, "Jules, do you know what happened to the first set of tablets that Moses broke when he came down from Mt. Sinai and saw the chaos amongst our people?" I replied, "you mean the pieces, no I don't." He said, "they were placed in the Ark and taken with the new set of tablets to the promised land." Rabbi, further stated "That means that even broken pieces can be treated as holy." Not a day has gone by that I don't think about that statement. Each day is a struggle for peace of mind. I have good days and bad days. My gun is no longer at home by request of my case worker before I was discharged. I suspect that is a good thing.

I realize now that Hashem was looking after me on April 6, 2008, by changing my work out time and by intervening on November 21ST, 2013. I am fairly certain that I actually spoke to a Vietnam Veteran that morning. But then again, could it have been a message from Stuart? Oddly enough I cannot picture the gentleman's face. I may never know…

My son Daniel with me on the day I was released from the hospital.

Chapman Auto photos and correspondence:

From: Julian Wyatt <jhillelcwyatt@icloud.com
<mailto:jhillelcwyatt@icloud.com>>
Date: June 19, 2014, at 18:50:17 MST
To: "SamAyala@champmanchoice.com<mailto:SamAyala@
champmanchoice.com>" <SamAyala@champmanchoice.com
<mailto:SamAyala@champmanchoice.com>>
Subject: Justin Lenocker – November 21st, 2013 – Life saver

Good Evening Gentlemen,

My name is Julian Wyatt. I am a retired 30-year Navy Combat and Disabled Veteran. On November 21st, 2013, after my visit at Chapman Bell Road Imports, I turned myself over to the Veterans Administration Building, where I was later diagnosed with Post Traumatic Stress Disorder (PTSD).

I spent 436 days in Iraq and have always known that something changed while I was there and lost colleagues, but I never sought help.

On November 21st, for no specific reason, I planned to take my life but for some strange reason, I received a call from Justin letting me know a part I ordered came in. The part was a dip stick for my Mitsubishi Montero Sport.

The entire day was a blur. I don't even remember driving there. I got the part and while putting it in Justin appeared behind me in the parking lot and asked if I wanted to get my oil changed since I was there. I declined but he persisted. He asked where else would you go and get your car washed and vacuumed for the same price as any place else! I got the message because I could not justify going anywhere else. Justin conveyed the need for me to stay. I felt it.

I handed him my keys and as I walked into the lobby a Vietnam Veteran asked me how I was doing? I was wearing my "Iraq War Veteran" ball cap. I greeted him with "Welcome Home" a common phrase given to Vietnam Vets because they never received a warm welcome when they returned.

One thing led to another and the Veteran said he was going to a PTSD Counseling Session at the Veterans Administration. He looked up the number of the department, Jade/Opal Clinic and gave me the number. I never asked for it.

While in the lobby, for the first time in a long time I allowed myself to feel pain and grief. I called Jodie Lynn and said I was ready for help and that I had planned today to take my life. She met me at the VA and I was later admitted. I am now receiving weekly counseling and feeling better.

I tell you this story because Justin was the catalyst in saving my life that day. Guardian Angels do exist. From my family to yours, thank you, thank you, thank you.

Very respectfully and sincerely,

Julian Wyatt
MS Ed, MBA, PhD Candidate
Lieutenant Commander, USN (Ret.)
Bronze Star Recipient

(Receipt for work performed on November 21st, 2013)

(Outside Chapman Auto where the Vietnam Veteran stood)

(The lobby where I sat and the letter from Chapman Auto)

LIVE SIMPLY
always
DREAM BIG
BE GRACIOUS
LAUGH OFTEN
& LOVE MUCH

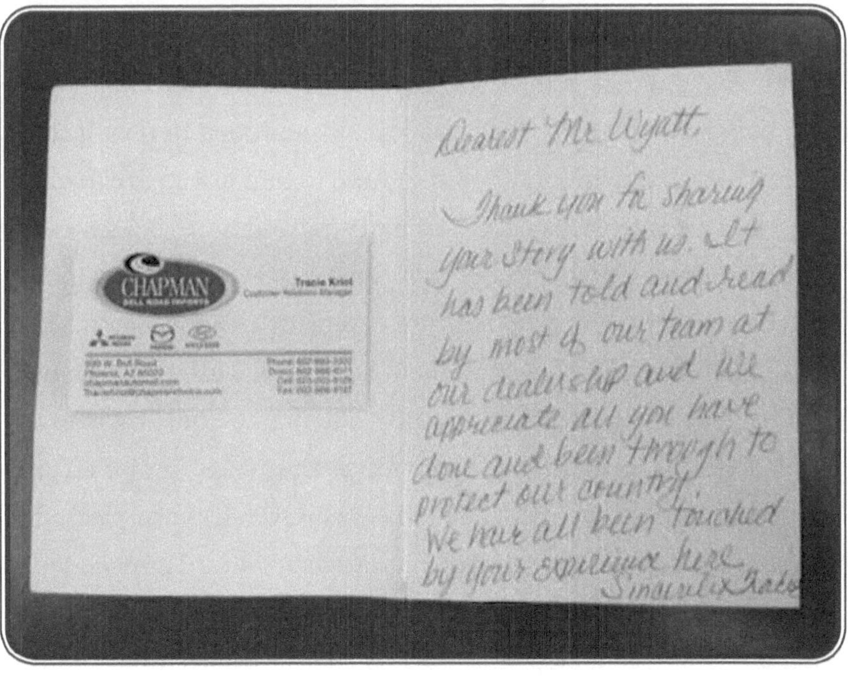
CHAPMAN
BELL ROAD IMPORTS
Tracie Kriel
Customer Relations Manager

Dearest Mr. Wyatt,

Thank you for sharing
your story with us. It
has been told and read
by most of our team at
our dealership and we
appreciate all you have
done and been through to
protect our country.
We have all been touched
by your experience here.
Sincerely, Tracie

(Thank you)

Closing thoughts

I returned from Iraq angry, displaced, burned out, chronically fatigued, depressed and I felt like I didn't belong here. This life was not the real life. Everyone walking around had no clue what life was all about and it made me violently sick to my stomach to see people having a good time or worse, arguing or debating something minor. I still have nightmares or rather flashbacks of hearing "Warning, Warning, take cover, incoming rounds." The sounds of helicopters remind me of Iraq. Insomnia plaques me. I can smell the burning garbage and relive the sweltering heat with each dream, waking up in a pool of sweat.

I honestly don't think I will ever be normal again. Things that are really important in my life have faded. I don't really enjoy anything anymore, so I stay busy, as busy as I can, to resist the stationary position at all costs, so my mind does not have a chance to wander. Therapy on another note, is going well and is long overdue.

Six months after the date that I finally admitted to myself that I needed help, I returned to Chapman Auto to find Justin, to explain to him what my intentions were that morning and how "he" saved my life. The photos above and the correspondence with them will stay with me forever. Every encounter we have with a person, could be the last. Look for signs…hold on to them because you just never know…

The journey has been an exciting one. I have come close to the brink of death more than once and I have experienced profound grief as well as happiness in the past 60 years. Overall, I am pleased at where I have arrived. My self-help regimen consists of Transcendental Meditation 2x per day for 20 minutes and Mussar training. The 18 middot, or rather character traits are listed below. Each trait is worked on for 1 week with a journal delineating the experience. I absolutely love it and if you are not familiar with it, I highly recommend visiting http:///www.mussarleadership.org/practice.html. The traits are:

Equanimity (Menuchat ha-nafesh)

Patience (Savlanut)

Order (Seder)

Decisiveness (arizuH)

Cleanliness (Nekiyut)

Humility (Anavah)

Righteousness (Tzedek)

Frugality (Keemutz)

Zeal/Diligence (Zeizut)

Silence (Shtikah)

Calmness (Nichutah)

Truth (Emet)

Separation (Prishut)

Temperance (Histapkut)

Deliberation (Mitenut)

Modesty (Tzniut)

Trust (Bitachon)

Generosity (Nedivut)

My safety plan while I was in the hospital has been a talisman over the past year and is submitted below:

Safety Plan

Step 1: <u>What are my warning signs?</u> Anxiety attack, tunnel vision, increased feeling of hopelessness, putting things in order, death looks better than living, wanting to be alone, etc.

Step 2: <u>What are my Internal coping strategies?</u> Things I can do to take my mind off my problems without contacting another person: Think about how my family and friends will feel, how school children will feel about my loss of life, go to the gym, don't be alone, read, pray and talk with my Rabbi.

Step 3: <u>People and social settings that provide distraction:</u> Lynn, my son Daniel, my daughter Nicole, My Mom, Yoga and go to Barnes and Nobles.

Step 4: <u>People whom I can ask for help?</u> Rabbi Dean, Lynn, My Son, Nicole, My Mom, Tanya, Weeze.

Step 5: <u>Professionals or agencies I can contact during a crisis?</u> 1 (800) 273-8255; 1 (877) 927-8387

Step 6: <u>Making the environment safe:</u> No access to gun or pills

DSM IV: 309.81 (PTSD)

PTSD

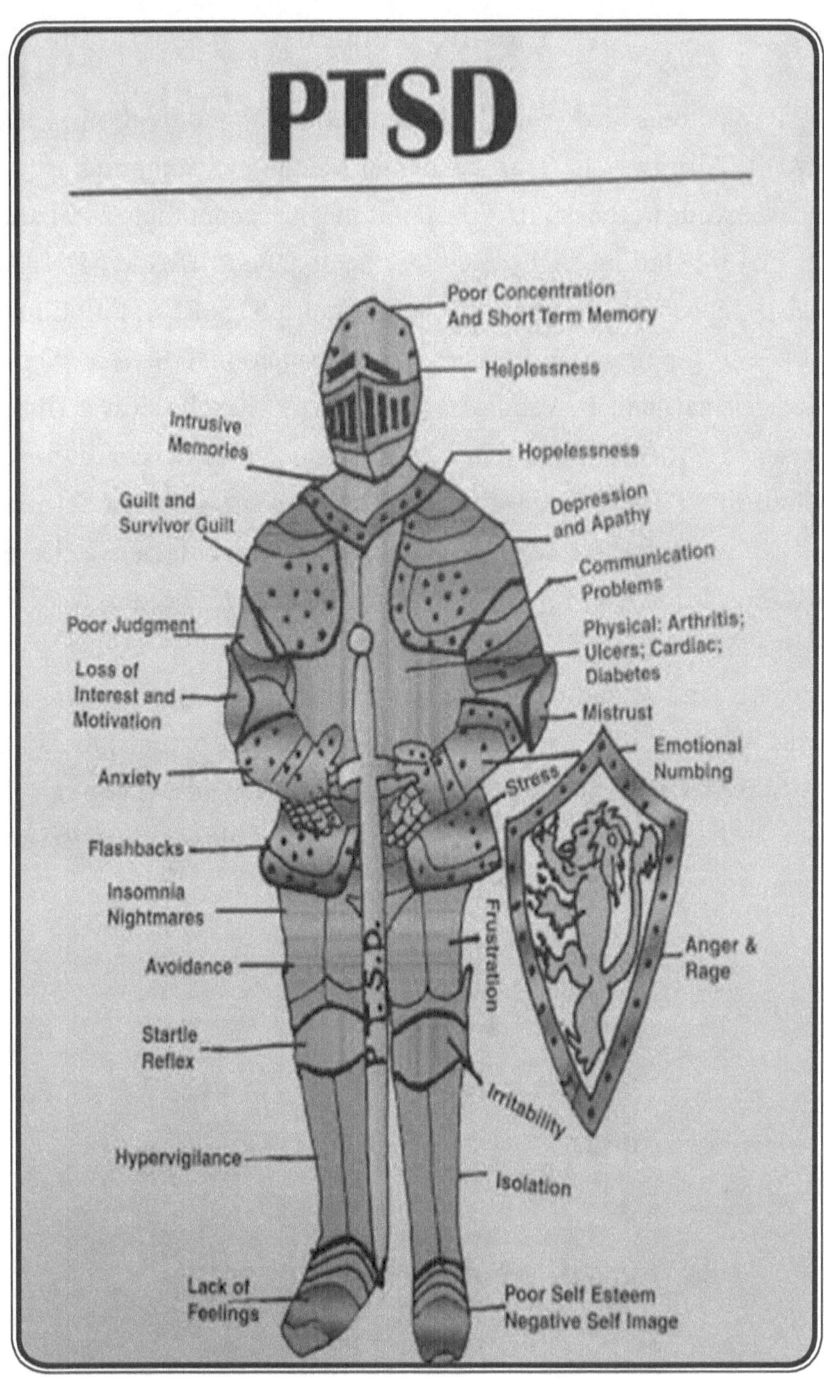

Lanham, S.L. (2007, pg. 14, Veterans and Families
Guide to Recovering from PTSD

Closing Thoughts

PTSD tools I've tried include: Frequency modulation, CBT, EMDR, Allergy tests, Transcendental Meditation, Acupuncture to include seeds in the ear, trigger point massage, cupping, Sacral and Cranial unwinding, Ashwagandha, Lemon Balm Extract, DHEA, Gaba, Liposomal Vitamin C with multiple SSRI's, Emotional Freedom Tapping (EFT), Yoga, Transformational Breath Work, Medical marijuana, Ayahuasca, Yage', Hape', Kambo, Kava, IRest, Presence Process, Ayurveda, Mushrooms, MBSR, Counseling, Mindfulness training, Japa meditation, Healing crystals, Selenite sticks, Tuning forks, essential oils (vetiver), Cranial Massage Release, Jose Silva Mind Control Method, Earthing mat, Bio Feedback, ACT, Emotionally Focused Couples Therapy, Reiki, etc.

"We want so badly to share our innermost experience with our loved ones, but often, we forget that not everyone can go where we go. Indeed, we all share this mysterious fact – that no one else can go into our depth completely. We must travel these alone. It is where we commune with God." Mark Nepo

CHAPTER ELEVEN

INDIVIDUAL AUGMENTEE FEEDBACK

*W*ithin one month of returning from Iraq, I typed the following letter and shared it with my organization:

16 December 2008

SUBJECT: SUPPORT / EXPERIENCE OF INDIVIDUAL AUGMENTEE (IA) ONBOARD PCU GEORGE H.W. BUSH (CVN 77); ICO LCDR JULIAN WYATT

BACKGROUND:

I received official notification as the "Alternate" IA candidate during the latter part of August 2007. The required core competency/designator was an Aviation or Surface Ordnance Limited Duty Officer (I am a surface ordnance designator).

From official receipt of orders to execution, I had 8 days with which to prepare for deployment. The location and execution of the orders were for Baghdad, Iraq, 436 days. I departed PCU BUSH (CVN 77) on 7 Sep 07, commenced initial training at NMPS Norfolk (10-17 Sep 07), followed by Army Boot Camp at Fort Riley, Kansas (18 Sep 07 – 30 Nov 07), attended an additional 1-week of training in Kuwait (2-9 Dec 07) and reported to Multi-National Security Transition Command – Iraq (MNSTC-I) on 10 Dec 07, as an advisor to the Joint Head Quarters Ammunition Directorate. I departed Iraq on 31 Oct 08, spent 1 week of decompression in Kuwait, and arrived in Norfolk, Va., on 4 Nov 08.

<u>DISCUSSION:</u>

The objective of this point paper is merely to capture and report my IA experience to the Executive Officer.

(1) IA Notification.

The process of notification for the IA; initially came from SURFPAC IA Coordinator and trickled down to PCU BUSH IA Coordinator (LCDR Hurd, AO, PCU BUSH). My Department Head, CDR Terhune was involved in the process early, which helped to dispel rumors. Both the Commanding Officer and Executive Officer spoke to me at length regarding the tour of duty, both professionally and personally. I had a farewell and an Engineering Department farewell.

(2) IA Processing at PCU BUSH and ECRC, Detachment Norfolk.

All paperwork, to include the duplicate record that was constructed for this process, was phenomenal. From medical and dental screening aboard, to NKO courses, Powers of Attorney, pay, etc., were professional and expeditious. As a program coordinator (3M), Cheng identified a relief early in the process which allowed time for me to draft a detailed POA&M and brief the XO and Commanding Officer regarding a short range and long-range plan, to include turnover of all collateral duties. The only paperwork that became confusing and was not included in the shipboard package was for "family separation allowance," to include who would start and stop it (ECRC versus the Ship). I brought this to the ship's attention and came back to the ship to have this signed. In regard to the pay beginning, I had to call the ship from Kuwait to start the process.

(3) Training pipeline.

I attended 90 days of training at Fort Riley, Kansas, which was more than sufficient. The training was geared toward IA's that are living and training with the Iraqi's. Everything from convoy operations to counter-insurgency operations and combat lifesaving qualifications, it was very in depth. Many of the skills were not utilized, but overall, it was not lacking in any capacity.

(4) IA Support during tour of duty.

Two perspectives are offered: one from the sailor aboard PCU BUSH and the other from my Family. As a sailor attached to PCU BUSH, I found the system to be more of a "pull" system, vice a "push" system. Meaning, when I contacted the ship (pulling), the reply was always within 48 hours or less. My Department Head routinely kept in contact with me, to include when anyone within Engineering Department was assigned to an IA, more specifically Iraq, the Cheng put me or rather them, in contact, to establish a network of support. All correspondence with LCDR Hal Mohler, AO, was absolutely phenomenal. From a family perspective, my fiancé and children were not contacted directly by the ship. But with that said, Lynn sent a monthly update to the Cheng, XO, CO, CMC and several others regarding my tour of duty with photos. The 1st LT, a very close friend of mine, CDR Glen Bourque, did however stay in constant contact with my family and at least on one occasion, came to my home and did a lot of yard work. I would like to mention that my department did send a gift box and a signed poster of the ship, which I proudly displayed in my work area.

(5) Tour of duty.

I found the overall tour of duty in Iraq to be extremely rewarding, both professionally and personally. I had a unique opportunity to work with coalition forces and host nationals, as well as conduct high level briefings (1-2 Star Generals), hone my skills as a leader in a dynamic and changing environment and engage in Nation Building. I resided in trailers and took a bus to and from work every day. Standard everyday outfit consisted of the desert camouflage uniform, a 9MM, M4 riffle with combat load, body armor and helmet. My Department Head was a USAF COL and my boss was a 1-Star General, Brigadier General Johnny Torrens-Spence. Quality Work Life was difficult with the OPTEMPO, 15+ hour days. Gym facilities and the Dining Facility (DFAC) were above adequate at the Forward Operating Base (FOB), where I was attached. While on assignment, I had one, 2-week leave period. During that time, Engineering Department Khaki's met me for a half-way mark celebration. Would I do it again? Absolutely!

(6) Reintegration.

In Kuwait, we spent one week decompressing. We filled out a very detailed assessment, which identified areas of concern, especially for those that lost colleagues or engaged the enemy. I lost two colleagues while deployed and survived over 1,000 rocket and mortar attacks. Upon return to the States, November 4th, 2008, I flew into Atlanta, GA. The troops were overwhelmed with support from the USO and

American's, waving flags, shaking our hands and clapping. It felt good to be home. Within 72 hours I reported to PCU BUSH and dropped off both my FITREP and End of Tour Award – Bronze Star. I took three weeks of leave. Upon return, I commenced turnover with the acting 3MO (same person I initially turned over with) and then briefed the XO on all concerns regarding the program. I felt 3 weeks was enough time.

RECOMMENDATION:

Assign a sponsor to every IA, ideally someone within the individual's Department. The sponsor would check-in with the IA and his or her family on a monthly basis to check on their welfare, to ascertain if they have heard from the service-member at all, etc. Additionally, the sponsor can fill the IA sailor in on basic shipboard /departmental information. The goal is to ensure the IA sailor does not feel as if h/she has been abandoned, which I did not.

Involve the Command Ombudsman in the process of checking in on the family, especially during holiday periods, beginning of school, birthdays, etc. The goal is to surround the family with an ethic of care – ensure that they too, do not feel abandoned.

During the reintegration phase (reporting back to the command), the IA sailor could fill out a form with a few questions (items of interest for the Command) as a method of improving the IA experience aboard PCU BUSH and feedback this information to ECRC, Departments, Ombudsman, CMC, etc. . Invite the IA personnel to provide critical feedback of the process.

During the reintegration phase (reporting back to the command), an additional check-in sheet, whereby the sailor meets with the CMC, XO, CO, Medical and Family Services to discuss any issues they may have or any issues that may have transpired (a lot of IA personnel go through divorces, have deaths in the family while deployed, etc.).

Continue to recognize those IA sailors as the Commanding Officer has done in the past at the Christmas Parties and maintaining a poster board that lists the location of our sailors on an IA. Use the IA sailors in whatever process that PCU BUSH develops.

Headed downrange, 2007

Bronze Star and All Services Worship

"Bronze Star presented by Brigadier General Johnny
Torrens-Spence, Baghdad, Iraq October 2008"

"…any man who may be asked in this century what he did to make his life
worthwhile, I think can respond with a good deal of pride and satisfaction:
I served in the United States Navy." President John F. Kennedy

CHAPTER TWELVE

Family comments

Comment from my Mom…Anne Kozdron

My Mr. Wonderful after his catholic education and many years in the US Navy and after researching and studying many different religions he knew where his heart lay and what resonated with him and it was Judaism.

I am so proud of the man that has emerged from this test of fire on the battleground of Iraq.

He came back stronger and more knowledgeable and more determined to be the best Jew he could be.

Having served 30 years in the navy and now retired he has finished the first of I hope many books to come

Hope you know how much I love you

Mom

Comment from my oldest sister: Tanya Wyatt

As a young man growing up Julian has always had the incredibly distinct gift of being able to interact with and inspire children. It is no wonder that his current interests engulf doing such that including writing a book about his experiences as a U.S. Navy service member whose roles comprise: grandfather, father, husband, brother, and uncle.

The first of three out of four siblings to join the U.S.Navy, his dedication to service and to our country has always been exemplary; especially when he was assigned unexpectedly to Iraq. As a Native and African American man of Jewish faith he held onto his teachings and encouraged, stimulated and motivated others to establish a circle that supported the Jewish faith and traditions even with the loss of one of their brothers, Maj Stuart Adam Wolfer.

As a sister and retired U.S. Navy member I could not be any prouder of his courage, honor and commitment in sharing his experiences with the world.

Very respectfully
CTO1 T.M. Wyatt, USN, Retired

Comment from my baby sister, Natasha L. Wyatt

Julian Wyatt… do you know this dude? His attitude is infectious… He is capable of being able to inspire you to leap parachute less into an active volcano and reassure you with back up plans, and blueprints in 3D and have you believe that you will land on your feet because he said he has faith in you and was willing to hold your hand thru it….

For some reason I always imagined him to be a mix between Kindergarten cop and the motivation speaker in a locker room of professional athletes offering everything that he's got just before game time....

He is dedicated, charismatic, tireless, awesome, loyal, protective, funny, intelligent, loving, moody, fearless, intuitive, focused, accepting, non-judgmental, sensitive, courageous, honest, generous, competitive, spiritual and so much more....

Anything you read from him is a mind journey with the vortex of your 3rd eye opening up. He is the leading light, the arrow on the sign that says go that way and he is such a breadth of fresh air that he makes Febreeze smell bad and such a perfectionist at times even bleached clothes seems dingy around him and will apologize before you notice...

Bruce Lee is quoted as stating "if you want to be immortal live a life worth remembering" and Julian was immortal the day he was born...

Living the life worthy of all kinds of accolades! He is a lot of things to a lot of people but to me he is my brother, my muse, my mentor, someone who would go to the end of the earth to protect your dignity and honor Julian is a luminary..... Yup! That's MY brother Julian! Aka Mr. Wonderful ☺ NLWJ aka Jamie Bond

Me, Natasha, Tanya and Jason Wyatt

CHAPTER THIRTEEN

Various photos

Chanukah in one of Sadaam Hussein's palaces, 2007)

(Tigress river in Iraq, Tashlich prayers)

(Mail call, Baghdad, Iraq, 2007-2008)

Facing six directions while shaking the lulav and etrog

Succot in Baghdad, Iraq, 2008

(CDR Rich Makarski, 2008)

(Day of departure from Iraq, November 2008)

(Passover in Iraq, 2008)

(Baghdad, Iraq, 2008, going away party for Maj. Robbins)

nd Welcomes
to our
Seder 5786
LEONARD
U.S. NAVY

U.S. ARMY
U.S. ARMY

(Purim, Baghdad, Iraq)

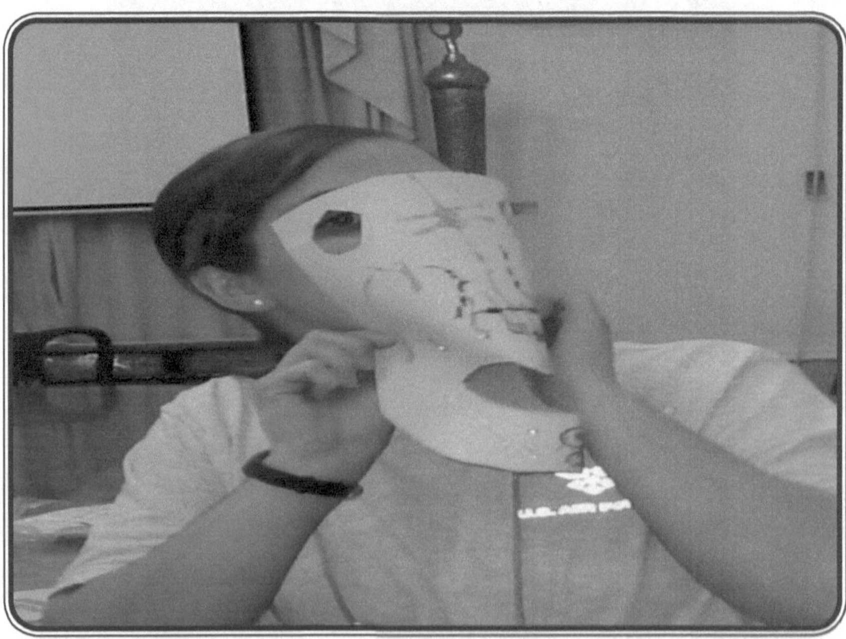

(Succot in Iraq, 2008)

(Cross swords, 2008, Baghdad, Iraq) Multinational
Security Transition Command - Iraq

(First night of Chanukah, Laveen, AZ, 2013)

(Father and Daughter in Iraq, 2008; safe and sound, lucky me)

(Laveen, Arizona, smoking a cigar, 2014)

(Iraq, with Nicole…my daughter)

(Selling Poppy seeds as part of the Jewish War Veterans, Post 619)

(My Navy shadow box)

Retirement ceremony: Captain DeWolfe Miller, Gabby, Rick, Lynn, Tanya, CDR Jason Wyatt, Natasha Johnson, Me, and my two little ones in front, Nathan and Alicia – July 8, 2010, USS George H.W. Bush (CVN 77)

(2007, Gloucester, Virginia, with a young Alicia)
Blessing her on Shabbat

(2009, Me with CW04 Danny Rogers)

(2013, Trailside Point School with Mr. Mark Trombino.
No place for Hate designation)

(2013, High Holidays)

(2013, Jewish War Veteran Induction Ceremony)

(2012, Gabby, me, Nicole with Payton, Derrez and Diana)

CDR Pete Bachand, Baghdad, Iraq 2007

Me, Khalida and Ashley, 2007-2008

Me, CDR Bachand, SGT Brandon Watts and our General

CDR Charmaine Savage, LT Steve Wilkerson and Me, 2007

Me with Iraqi Counterpart, 2007

M9, M4 and Cigar!

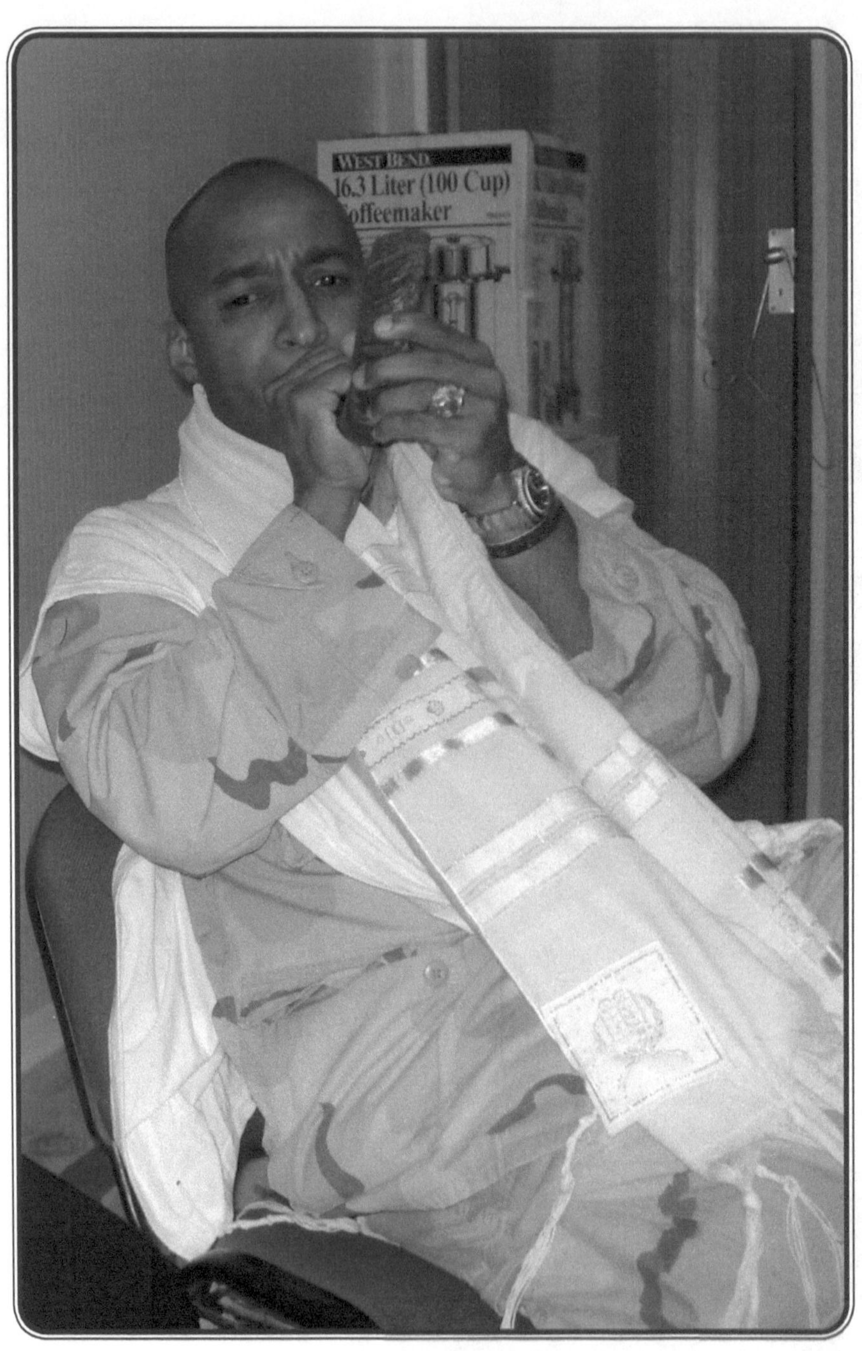

Jewish New Year, Blowing the Shofar

Colonel Scott and Maj. Wolfer, in memory, 2008, Baghdad, Iraq

Presidential letters of appreciation for retirement

Baghdad Cigar Aficionado Club

Commissioning Ceremony, USS George H.W. Busch (CVN77)

ENDORSEMENT

*O*rganizations that I proudly endorse include but are not limited to:

Major Stuart Adam Wolfer Institute (MSAWI), which is committed to supporting US Troops stationed abroad through Dandelion Projects – MSAWI needs to be on your "check-out sheet" for those that receive overseas orders; **Hospice of the Valley**, where you conduct Shabbat Service for Jewish patients in their homes and perform the Salutes Program for Veterans; **Jewish War Veterans**, where you can play a vital role in your community to positively impact the lives of others; **LinkedIn Jewish Professionals Group**, where you can network with other Jewish personnel; and visit the local **Jewish Community Center** (JCC). You can also "google" top Jewish Profit/Non-Profit Organizations and look for those in your area. **Mindfulness First** has been a true life saver for me. Please visit the website to read about the work we are doing in the schools, it's transformational! One of the best decisions I have ever made was to become a registered yoga teacher (RYT-500), Vinyasa Yoga.

The practice has enabled me to move into stillness and reconnect with feeling safe, grounded and comfortable. I have become a huge fan of the following books:

— The Living Gita by Sri Swami Satchidananda
— Yoga Nidra by Swami Satyananda Saraswati
— The Yamas & Niyamas by Deborah Adele
— The spirit and practice of moving into stillness by Erich Schiffmann

— The Path of the Yoga Sutras by Nicolai Bachman
— How Yoga Works by Geshe Michael Roach
— Light on Yoga by B.K.S. Iyengar

I also enjoy Primordial Meditation! I use it in conjunction with Transcendental Meditation (TM). I still remember the day I was given my personal mantra. A real game changer with regards to establishing inner peace. Michael A. Singer, "The Untethered Soul" is a must read if you want to understand your Inner Critic and silencing him/her. Powerful book!

To My Partner, My Darling Lisa Dodi Li – My Beloved is Mine

May 14th, 2019: Still holding hands

Will you marry me? April 14, 2019

My wedding was performed by Pastor Earnest Fitzhugh at Redemption Life Center Church in Phoenix, AZ., under the Chuppah.

April, 14th, 2019
and
May 14th, 2019

My Darling,

I remember this day as if it were yesterday. The planning, the recruitment of our daughter, Diana; son, Jackson; and close friends. I was so excited to put my military uniform back on, with medals and walk through the restaurant (Compass, downtown Phoenix), towards you. Just like a scene out of "An Officer and a Gentleman." I will never forget, kneeling, removing my cover and pulling out my speech, that ended with will you marry me.

Fast forward to one month later, standing underneath the Chuppah, I read the following words to you in front of G-d and the community in attendance:

"There is a scene in The Divine Comedy, the narrative poem by Dante written in Italian circa 1308–21, where Dante is met by Beatrice, and the description is as follows...embodying the knowledge of divine mysteries bestowed by Grace, who leads him through the successive ascending levels of heaven to the Empyrean, where he is allowed to glimpse, for a moment, the glory of God.

Lisa, your love has colored all that I experience with such a profound sense of beauty and a nearness to G-d that I have never experienced in a relationship. The day you entered my life, a million points of light shattered the darkness.

I am most humbled by your love and how I've changed as a result of it. Thank you for helping me to breathe again. You are my

Beatrice and I willingly and eagerly await our magnificent future. Thank you for loving me so completely and unconditionally. You have single handedly reminded me that true love is possible and it is my turn to be truly happy."

Darling,

From the very beginning, you asserted yourself in my healing process. It began with couples counseling with Connie at the Vet Center, where we had joint sessions and one-on-one.

It continued to include your physical presence at all of my VA appointments, especially with my Mental Health Doctor, Mark Harp. You ensured my medications were up-to-date and helped me to get on a good schedule.

You signed up for the Caregiver program and PTSD course designed for spouses! You never cease to amaze me. The fact that you knew I was also Bi-polar before that diagnosis was even rendered and finally placed on the right medications, is amazing.

My true healing began with you because you refused to see me fail over and over again. I owe you a debt of gratitude that I will be hard pressed to ever repay. Thank you for not giving up on me Luv. You are my navigator, my true north, leading me back to love, where I am safe and secure. I love you with all my heart and soul. Mama, your feedback on this manuscript was extremely helpful and I appreciate you. Finally, I can say one of my favorite words in Hebrew, "Hineni" – Here I am!

Eternally yours,

Love,

Juju

BY <u>E. E. CUMMINGS</u>

i carry your heart with me, i carry it in
my heart

i am never without it, anywhere
i go you go ~ my dear; and whatever is done by only me, is your doing,
my darling.

i fear no fate, for you are my fate ~
my sweet.

i want no world, for beautiful, you are my world, my truth and you are
whatever a moon has always meant and whatever a sun will always
sing is you.

here is the deepest secret nobody knows,
here is the root of the root and the bud of the bud.

and the sky of the sky of a tree called life; which grows higher than
soul can hope or mind can hide, and this is the wonder that's keeping
the stars apart.

i carry your heart, i carry it in my heart.

This is my family: May 14th, 2019

"Authentic success is feeling good about who you are, appreciating where you've been, celebrating your achievements, and honoring the distance you've already come.

Authentic success is reaching the point where "being" is as important as "doing." It's the steady pursuit of a dream. It's realizing that no matter how much time it takes for a dream to come true in the physical world, no day is ever wasted. It's valuing inner, as well as outer, labor – both your own and others. It's elevating labor to a craft and craft to an art by bestowing Love on every task you undertake."

Sarah Ban Breathnach, *Simple Abundance*

My mom passed away on July 4th, 2020 before the publishing of this manuscript. It was her dream as well as mine to complete this project. This is for you Mom.

I have changed the title of this book at least half a dozen times over the past seven years. "Becoming Jewish" was the recommendation of my wife, because being Jewish is never fully accomplished. The study, the doing, is ongoing. I hope this body of work serves you. L'Shalom

Our practice of sitting back to back from childhood to now.
Thank you for capturing this moment Jodie Lynn.

Dedicated to Mom:

It was a beautiful Fourth of July in Whiting, N.J., this past Saturday in 2020. The temperature was 85 degrees for the high and 70 degrees for the low.

July's full moon occurs on Sunday, July 5, 2020 at 12:44 a.m., but the moon appeared the fullest the night before, July 4th, and after its peak to the casual stargazer. <u>July's full moon</u> is known as the Buck Moon, though it has many other nicknames by different cultures.

Mom, Anne W.B. Kozdron, of blessed memory, chose the Buck moon to light her way home with fireworks!

Mom was born on Sunday, September 24th, 1933 in Worcester, Mass and she was escorted home by her sisters, husband and parents on Saturday, July 4th, 2020.

Mom was in hospice care in her home in Whiting, N.J., from Thursday, July 2nd through Saturday July 4th., she was 87 years old.

My siblings Tanya, Jason and Natasha were standing at her bedside when she drew her last breath. I was called at 10:29pm last night. Ironically, I was born at 10:29am on July 8th.

We recited the 23rd Psalm, we read A Woman of Valor poem (Proverb 31) and the Mourners Kaddish.

Upon hearing the news I rended (tore) my shirt out of physical anguish and despair (Jewish custom).

I can't stop the tears from falling. You are the only one who truly understands me. I have a lifetime of memories from this woman. Be it, climbing a fence and taking a short cut through a cemetery with paper bags of groceries (a bad idea), to mailing cans of food and cereal when I was enlisted and money was tight, to holding Christmas for my sailors in a hotel in 1980, and the incessant jokes at every call; I will miss you more than I can say Mom. My heart is broken. I have lost my best friend. You were such a lady and a collector of people. I look forward to the day of reuniting with you, my first love.

The Watch; Naval Tradition.

In our Navy tradition, when someone retires, we read a poem called "The watch." I have changed it, for a tribute in honor of my Mom, Anne Kozdron, and siblings, Tanya, Jason and Natasha.

I know that everyone that knew my Mom is mourning. She was just that kind of lady.

Yes, Family and Friends,

For many years, Anne Kozdron has stood the watch.

While some of us lay about sleeping at night, my Mom, stood the watch.

While others of us were attending schools, Ms.'s Wonderful (our nicknames for each other) stood the watch. And yes, even before many of us were born, my Mom stood the watch with crazy humor and always an empathetic ear with great advice, she maintained the watch.

For many years my Mom stood the watch; often times putting others needs above her own; So that her family and friends could sleep soundly, in safety, shelter and protection, knowing that no matter what, She would continue to stand the watch. From all of Moms acts of kindness, Role modeling how a woman of Valor contributes to society and family, and so proud of our Native American Heritage; We are comforted knowing that a red rose is her sacred heart, A white rose is her face, and that her breath has turned this barren world to a rich and flowery place.

Mom is the rose of our collective hearts, her gardeners are we, and together, we shall drink her fragrance in the hearth of our love and memory, Where she will never die.

Grandfather North:

You are the warrior, you have ridden alongside my Mom, Natasha, Jason, Tanya, Me and all grandchildren, great grandchildren and extended family into battle. You have also felt their love and caring when you were wounded or lonely; ride along side of them, for now they are in the hardest battle for their life, the battle for inner peace. Now is the time for you to care for them.

Grandfather Sky:

May your songs of the winds and clouds sweep the pain and sadness out of all who loved her; as they hear those songs, let them know the spirit who are with those songs, are also at peace.

GrandMother Earth:

I have asked all the other Grandfathers and Grandmothers to help our family rid themselves of the troubles that way so heavily on their hearts. This way, the weight they carry will be less; and they will walk more softly upon you.

GrandMother Earth, from your womb all spirits have come and when they return to you; cradle them gently in your arms and allow them to join their loved ones in the skies. If they want to hurry themselves to you, tell them you are not ready; and they must wait, for now they can pass on peace to others.

To The Wyatt Family,

I believe Mom is always whispering,

Do not stand at my grave and forever weep, I am not there; I do not sleep. I am a thousand winds that blow. I am the diamond glints on snow. I am the sunlight on ripened grain. I am the gentle autumn's rain. When you awaken in the morning's hush, I am the swift uplifting rush. Of quiet birds in circled flight, I am the soft stars that shine at night. Please, do not stand at my grave and forever cry. I am not there. I did not die.

Today, we are here to say Mom, Auntie, Gigi, Grandmother, Friend to many;

The Watch stands relieved. Relieved by those you have given advice, mentored, sacrificed, and loved the only way you know how - completely and all consuming with humor.

Mom, you now stand relieved. We, your family and friends, have and will carry on the watch."

With all the love I have,

I remain,

Your Proud & Grateful Son.

www.ingramcontent.com/pod-product-compliance
Lightning Source LLC
Chambersburg PA
CBHW031015190726
48286CB00003BA/850